A CASE FOR DISCRETION

By the Author

Love in the Limelight

A Case for Discretion

A CASE FOR DISCRETION

by

Ashley Moore

2024

A CASE FOR DISCRETION

ISBN 13: 978-1-63679-617-8

This Trade Paperback Original Is Published By
Bold Strokes Books, Inc.
P.O. Box 249
Valley Falls, NY 12185

First Edition: April 2024

CREDITS
EDITOR: JENNY HARMON
PRODUCTION DESIGN: STACIA SEAMAN
COVER DESIGN BY TAMMY SEIDICK

Acknowledgments

I would like to thank everyone who listened to me go on and on about this book as I wrote it. I would particularly like to thank AnnaKatherine, Barb, and Michelle. My mom also read (almost) all of this while I was writing it, and she was always there to ask clarifying questions when she didn't understand why a character was acting in a specific way. She made the book better with her questions. My editor, Jenny Harmon, is the best, most supportive editor ever. I know every author says that, but they're all incorrect and I'm right. Jenny is awesome.

I would also like to thank everyone who read my first book. I wouldn't be here without people reading and enjoying it. I hope everyone enjoys this one too.

PROLOGUE

Gwen rolled her neck out and looked through the large window that took up one wall of her open-plan condo. Atlanta sprawled out in front of her, endless lights reflected back at her in the glass. Even though she was in the building's penthouse, the building itself wasn't quite tall enough to see where the lights ended. Other skyscrapers interrupted her view. The highways snaked around and cut through the city, and for a moment, she got lost in the flow of traffic below her. By this time of night, the perpetual gridlock of the day had eased into a regular stream of drivers, busy, but still moving.

"Are you bringing us that wine or not?" a voice called out across the room. Judith, never Judy, her eldest sister, always had been impatient. Gwen finished uncorking the second bottle of wine they were going to indulge in that night. She refilled their glasses.

A shared dinner had come and gone and now she, Judith, and Lillian, the middle sister of the three, were lounging comfortably in Gwen's living room. The three of them had dinner almost every month, normally a light affair where they bitched about their significant others, or in her case her lack of a significant other, or talked about their children. This time, it wasn't the lack of a partner that Gwen had on her mind.

She walked into the living room and handed each of her sisters a glass. Lillian smiled in thanks, but Judith pinned Gwen with a knowing look.

"So, what terrible thing has happened that you don't want to tell us about?" Judith cocked her head to the side and looked at Gwen.

"What? Nothing. Nothing bad has happened." Gwen shook her head. The denial was automatic. "Where did that idea come from?" Sometimes, she hated that Judith knew her so well. She wondered what exactly had given away her nervousness. Normally, she had a better poker face.

Judith gave her a flat look. "You've been acting squirrelly all night. The last time you were like this was when you told us you were divorcing David. So, forgive me if I think you're about to tell us something equally life changing."

"You're being absurd." Gwen turned to Lillian for support.

"Don't look at me. I agree with her. Something's up." Lillian looked at Gwen over the top of her glasses. Gwen loved her sisters, she did, but sometimes they were too perceptive.

Gwen huffed and collapsed onto the couch next to Lillian but was careful not to spill her wine. "All right, fine. There was something I wanted to talk to you about. But it isn't bad. I'm not getting another divorce."

"Hard to get a divorce when you aren't married," Judith commented dryly. Gwen shot her a look that said her sense of humor wasn't appreciated. Judith shrugged.

"Fine. If you'd give me a moment, I'd tell you." As the youngest of the three sisters, sometimes it was hard to get a word in edgewise, particularly if Judith got on about something.

"Yes, yes." Judith waved her wine glass imperiously. Even though it was Gwen's condo, somehow Judith made it seem like she was the one in charge and Lillian and Gwen were merely her subjects. Gwen had never been quite sure how she did that.

Gwen paused for another moment. She had a feeling that once she put this into words, put it into the universe, everything would change. "There's a rumor going around that Justice Carmichael is retiring soon. He isn't going to run again. He isn't even going to finish out his term." Gwen looked at her sisters significantly.

"It's about time," Lillian said. "He's what? In his nineties? He's a relic."

"He's eighty-one, which isn't the point. The point is the seat will be empty." Gwen wondered if they would put her implications together.

Judith looked at her shrewdly, eyes narrowed and lips in a thin line. "You want the governor to appoint you to replace him, don't you?"

"I do." It was a simple statement, but if she went through with it, it would change everything. Gwen steeled herself for their objections. She knew Judith, at least, would have questions. She would think of things that Gwen hadn't.

"You're not a judge," Judith pointed out. "And you'll have to face an election to keep the appointment. You haven't run for any sort of office since you lost that election for student body president in twelfth grade."

"Neither of those are requirements to be appointed," Gwen replied. Those objections she had been ready for. She knew she had weaknesses as a candidate. She was confident she could overcome them.

"You'll have challengers. The appointing commission has thirty-five people on it. You'll need to convince most of them," Judith went on.

"I can do that." Gwen might be worried about how her family would respond to her ambitions, but she had complete faith in her ability to accomplish her goal. She couldn't force the commission to recommend her, but she could make it damned hard for them to ignore her.

Judith gave her another searching look. She took a sip of her wine while Gwen waited for her next pronouncement. She would apply whether or not her sisters supported her, but she wanted them in her corner.

Judith nodded slowly. "I like it." There was a ruthlessness to her grin.

With Judith settled, Gwen turned to Lillian.

Lillian looked at her fondly. "You know you have my support. When does this all become official?"

"Carmichael's supposedly making the announcement before

the start of the April term. The governor will want to appoint someone before the December term." Gwen had already done her research. She knew how everything should play out. She could see the future stretched out in front of her. There were a million things she needed to do, but for now, she was going to enjoy her wine and her sisters' company.

"Well, then." Judith met Gwen's eyes. "Let's have a toast to the next justice on the Georgia State Supreme Court." She raised her glass.

"Hear, hear," Lillian said as she tapped her glass against Judith's.

Gwen let a grin spread across her lips. She reached out with her glass as well, and the sound of them tapping against each other rang though her living room. This wasn't going to be easy, but she had never chosen the easy way out before. This was no time to start.

❖

"Well, did you get the job?" Etta's mother asked over the phone without bothering to say hello.

Etta sighed and hoped her mother didn't hear her.

"I don't know. They're probably interviewing twenty people." It wasn't what her mother wanted to hear, but it was the only thing Etta could tell her. Summer associate positions at firms as prestigious as Dunleavy Byrd were highly competitive.

"Well, hopefully you impressed them. I don't need to tell you how important this summer is for you. If you want to work there after you graduate, then you need to get this job," Etta's mother said.

Etta wasn't sure Dunleavy Byrd was where she saw herself after she graduated, but sometimes it was easier to give in to her mother's expectations. A summer associate position wasn't forever. The summer would come and go and then she would decide just how much she wanted to rebel with her choice of careers. Maybe she would even like Dunleavy Byrd. Maybe she would be able to see her future there.

"You'll call me after they've offered you the job?" That her mother would be incredibly disappointed in her if they didn't offer her the job went unspoken between them.

"I will, Mom." For now, Etta wanted off the phone. It was an hour and a half to get back home, and she couldn't take her suit off until she got there. She didn't want to spend the drive defending all of her life choices from her mother's scrutiny. She wanted to zone out until she got back. Her friends were going out that night, and she had every intention of going with them, but she needed to get home at a reasonable time first.

"All right," her mother said. Etta could tell her mind was already on something else. "I'll talk to you later."

"I love you," Etta said. She might be annoyed, but never forgot to tell her mother that she loved her.

"I love you too," her mother echoed.

"Bye." Etta ended the phone call with an emphatic tap on her phone's screen. She knew the amount of pressure she used didn't matter, but it made her feel a tiny bit better. Talking to her mother was always an exercise in frustration. It didn't matter what she wanted. It only mattered what her mother wanted. Anything else was irrelevant.

Still, a summer associate position at Dunleavy Byrd would come with an embarrassingly excessive salary, one that she needed. Scholarships might cover her tuition, but there wasn't much left over for living expenses. She'd had to take out loans. A summer at a big firm would have her set for the year. Thirty-five thousand dollars for ten weeks' worth of work was absurd, but her bank account couldn't afford for her to say no if they offered her the job.

Etta took a deep breath as she turned onto the on-ramp. She would be home soon enough. For now, she would put the interview from her mind. She had done the best she could to impress the recruiter. The final decision was up to somebody else.

CHAPTER ONE

G wen stepped into the Bear's Den with trepidation. Named after the university's mascot, the place hadn't existed when she had gone to school there, and she couldn't imagine that an on-campus bar would be up to her standards. Still, it was the only place in the vicinity where they could get food, or more realistically, a drink, without a twenty-minute debate about where to go.

Roosevelt University's Board of Trustees meeting had run late, and the committee meeting she'd had to attend after the full meeting had gone even later. They were supposed to be choosing the book that everyone on campus would be required to read in the fall. It wasn't the most onerous of the things Gwen had ever done for the university, but it still required attention and care.

The committee itself wasn't large, which was how she had ended up at the Bear's Den in the first place. If it *had* been a large committee, she could have begged off the post-session invitation to drinks without fear that she would miss an unofficial decision that occurred during her absence. But as there were only a few people on this committee, it would be strategically foolish to be the only one not in attendance.

Gwen winced as they walked into the bar and into a wall of sound. Whoever was singing wasn't atrocious, but they clearly weren't a professional either. As the group rounded the corner into the bar proper, Gwen saw why.

It was karaoke night.

She was in hell.

But she couldn't back out now. So, she followed one of the students on the committee to the side of the room and waited while they pulled two tables together. She thought the boy might be named Henry. She couldn't remember the girl's name at all, but she was desperately glad that her son wasn't on the committee. She loved Christian, but he would have been a nightmare to work with on something like this. Henry and what's-her-name pulled chairs up to the newly expanded table, and Gwen sat down as elegantly as she could at its head.

Ben slid into view next to her, and she wondered if her cousin's place on the committee was designed entirely to annoy her. He might be a professor at T.R., as the university was known colloquially, but there were well over a hundred other professors there who could have joined the committee instead of him.

"What are you drinking, Gwen?" he half shouted over the sounds of the singer. "I'll go get a round."

"A martini. Gin. With a twist," she enunciated carefully. She was probably going to end up with a monstrosity that was barely tolerable, but as long as the bartender managed not to put olive brine in it, she would consider it a success.

Ben looked like he was going to say something else, but at her glare, he put his hands up and backed away.

The other members of the committee took seats around the table and passed along their drink orders to Ben before he meandered over to the bar. Really, would it hurt him to move with a bit of purpose?

Now that she was settled, Gwen looked around more carefully. There was a small stage at the front of the room. The night's current entertainment was up there singing "Pour Some Sugar On Me." Opposite the stage was the bar where there were currently two bartenders working: a man, big and muscular, in a purple band T-shirt and a woman a full head shorter than him in a black tank top. For some reason, Gwen got stuck looking at the woman. Her long, brown hair was piled up in a messy bun on the top of her head. She had a white and blue striped wristband pushed up almost to her elbow on her left forearm. For some unknown reason, she was wearing red suspenders. She seemed to be nodding her head along with the music until Ben stepped up to her section of the bar and she leaned close to be able to hear the orders he was passing along. Gwen forced her gaze away from them and back to the table. She didn't want to get caught staring.

When she refocused her attention, she saw that what's-her-name (maybe Hillary?) had grabbed a giant black three-ring binder from another table and was flipping through it while Brynn, one of the chemistry professors, looked over her shoulder. Hillary pointed to something, and Brynn nodded before they found a sign-up slip and Hillary wrote something down on it. Gwen resisted the urge to rub her forehead. They were going to sing. This night was getting better and better. Henry was too far away from her to be able to comfortably make small talk with him, so Gwen sat silently.

She only had to wait in purgatory for a few minutes before Ben placed a crystal-clear drink in a martini glass in front of her. In the drink, there was a thick piece of lemon peel leaning against the side of the glass. She picked the drink up without waiting for Ben to finish putting everyone else's drinks down. The glass was shockingly cold against her fingers. A quick sniff left her with the scent of the lemon in her nose, and she took a small sip, prepared to be disappointed. Instead, she tasted bright juniper berries and smooth vermouth, perfectly balanced against each other and at just the right temperature. Swallowing, she immediately took another sip, this time letting her eyes close as she tasted the drink.

It was perfection. It was *certainly* better than she had expected out of this shoddy, student-staffed bar.

Gwen pinned Ben with a look. "Which of them made this?" She motioned toward the bar with her head.

"Now, Gwendolyn, don't go bite her head off because the gin doesn't live up to your standards," Ben replied.

Gwen glared at him before standing up. She took her martini with her as she walked over to the bar. It looked like the others were content to sing karaoke together while they drank cheap beer, but nothing about that sounded fun to Gwen. It would be rude to simply leave, so her next best option was to be near the source of the decent drinks. Luckily, there was a spot at the end of the bar where it turned a corner into the wall. Gwen pulled out the barstool and took a seat.

A few moments later, the female bartender appeared in front of her. "Is there something wrong with your martini?" She nodded toward Gwen's drink.

"The problem is with the company. The drink is superb." Gwen couldn't hold back the compliment, and she smiled when the girl blushed.

"Thank you." The girl wiped her hands on a bar towel and offered her hand to Gwen. "I'm Etta. Just wave me down when you're ready for another."

Gwen took Etta's hand and shook it. "Gwen. It's a pleasure."

"Great." Etta flashed a smile before turning back to fill another order.

With Etta gone, Gwen pulled out her phone to see if she had any messages. If anything had been truly urgent, her assistant would have called her, but there was still a chance that something less pressing would have come up. She checked her email first, but there was nothing there that couldn't wait until the next day. Her text messages were equally quiet, but there was a little red notification icon next to the group chat she was in with her sisters. She tapped it open only to find Judith and Lillian placing bets on how long she would last before she kicked Ben under a table. She replied that she couldn't kick him if they weren't at the same table, then closed the app.

She took another sip of her martini before opening her text messages again and navigating to the conversation she was having with Christian. She told him that her meeting had run late and that she was staying the night with Ben. When she didn't get an immediate reply, she invited him to breakfast the next morning and then put her phone away. There was no predicting how he might answer or when he might even see her text message, but the offer was there if he wanted to take her up on it.

Gwen went to take another sip of her martini only to find that it was empty. She frowned before looking up at the bartenders. They were both still filling orders, but Gwen raised a few fingers when

Etta looked her way, and she got a nod in acknowledgment. Gwen noticed that Etta had brown eyes and that she was looking at Gwen as if she knew something Gwen didn't.

The music changed from boy bands to something by Queen. Queen was not horrible as far as bands went, but Gwen doubted that anyone at a college bar on a Thursday night was any match for it. She sat in dread through the intro and then winced hard when the singer started. She had been correct. Whoever was singing really should have picked a different song.

"Yeah, he comes in here every week and pretends to be Freddie Mercury." Etta took away the empty glass.

"How do you stand it?" Gwen replied.

Etta smiled at her, and Gwen nearly got caught in her smile. "You get used to it. Would you like another martini?"

"Please." She pulled a card from her wallet and handed it over.

"Want to start a tab?" Etta asked.

"My cousin over there conveniently lives within stumbling distance of the university and I'm unexpectedly staying with him tonight, so I might as well live a little." It was too far to drive back to Atlanta that night, and Ben would never let her get a hotel room. For once, that was working in Gwen's favor. She could have as many of the unexpectedly good martinis as she wanted.

"Gin, with a twist, right?" Etta said as she handed the card back.

"Correct," Gwen replied.

This time when Etta made the drink, Gwen watched her. Etta started by chilling the glass before she pulled out the gin and a slightly dusty bottle of vermouth from a back cabinet. She carefully measured the ingredients into a mixing glass, stuck a bar spoon in it, and started swirling the ice around with the alcohol. Gwen was transfixed. Not by the chemistry, but by the flex and pull of the muscles in Etta's forearm. She tried to look at Etta's face instead, but the look of concentration there was equally distracting.

"So, what do you study when you aren't bartending?" Gwen tried for light conversation. If nothing else, it was better than listening to bad karaoke.

"Law," Etta said over her shoulder in Gwen's direction.

"Is Professor Brightman still teaching Con Law?" Gwen couldn't stop herself from asking.

"Yeah, she is. You're a lawyer?" Etta asked, though she didn't pay any more attention to Gwen than she had before, finishing Gwen's drink instead.

"I am," Gwen replied.

Etta finally poured the drink into a glass, then turned toward Gwen and placed it in front of her. "Here you go."

"Thank you." Gwen nodded before taking a sip. "Just as good as the last one. Tell me, how did you get so good at making martinis? Certainly, it wasn't in this place." Gwen looked around disdainfully.

Etta laughed. "This place isn't so bad. But you're right, I don't get many people in here ordering martinis. I bartended out in California for a while right out of college and at Fleur de la Mer in Atlanta for a hot second before starting law school."

Gwen knew the restaurant. "I've been there. I remember having some excellent sea bass. I never would have thought to sit at the bar, though."

"You don't seem like someone who often sits at bars when there's a dining room available. Except for here, of course, where you're sitting at the bar because it's the farthest place away from the music. And because you know I won't fuck up your drink." Etta's smile looked wicked, and Gwen wondered if she was flirting with her. She idly wondered just how much younger Etta was than her, but then, it didn't really matter. They might flirt a bit over martinis, but they were hardly going to start a relationship. It probably wouldn't progress beyond the flirting anyway.

"Mmm, that's true." Gwen took a sip of the new drink and closed her eyes as it slid down her throat. "Still, I should probably get back to the table. It's rude of me to abandon them just because I find the location questionable."

"Well, come back up when you're ready for another drink." Etta winked at Gwen, but before Gwen could reply, she turned toward someone else who was waving her down.

Gwen really didn't want to go back to the table but felt she needed to, so she made her way over and reclaimed her seat.

"Good of you to rejoin us," Ben said as he looked up at Gwen. "Has the bartender been suitably chastised for not having a gin you like?"

"I'm pretty sure the bartender is the only person in this bar worth talking to." Gwen rolled her eyes. She shouldn't have agreed to come with them to the bar, but now she was stuck.

"You wound me." Ben put his hand to his chest in mock affront. "If she's better company than us, then perhaps you should go back over there. We're hardly talking about anything groundbreaking. Brynn and Hillary are waiting for their turn at karaoke, and Henry and I are talking about his Japanese midterm. No one's going to make any decisions without you. Hell, you know where my spare key is. You could go back to the house and escape this torture chamber."

"When you put it like that, I think I will go back to the bar." Gwen should have just taken Ben up on his offer to head to his place, but she found she wasn't quite ready to do that. So she picked her drink back up and headed back to the bar. She retook her previous barstool and sipped at her martini.

"You've returned," Etta said as Gwen settled.

"I find your company to be superior to that of my companions," Gwen said dryly. "They're talking about midterms. It isn't a subject that interests me anymore. I'm long past the point of having to worry about such things."

"Not an academic, then? I mean, I suspected as much, since you're a lawyer but not on the law faculty. I suppose you could always be a visiting lecturer or the dean of one of the schools I don't know anything about." Etta shrugged.

"No, I'm on the board of trustees," Gwen said. "I'm an alum and my son goes to school here."

"Ah." Etta started pouring a beer from the tap, but her attention stayed on Gwen. "So not only are you a lawyer, you're the kind with more money than you know what to do with."

"Something like that," Gwen replied with a smile. "Though most of it is family money."

"Oh, of course." Etta's eyes sparkled with mirth. "But you couldn't possibly talk about it because that wouldn't be polite."

"No, it wouldn't be." Gwen smiled back at her.

"Do you need another drink?" Etta asked as she nodded toward Gwen's now empty glass.

"Do you make other things as well as you make martinis?" Gwen twisted the stem of her empty glass between her fingers. Etta plucked the glass away from her and filled a second glass with ice water before placing it down in front of Gwen.

"You should drink that, so you don't get a hangover." Etta pointed toward the water. "I'm a pretty good bartender, but I'm no mind reader. Did you have something you were thinking of?"

"I was hoping you might recommend something." Gwen leaned forward a little.

"Normally, if someone is drinking martinis, I try to push them toward a Martinez, but I definitely can't make one of those here." Etta smiled ruefully. "And I was leading you on a little. Truthfully, the only reason I have gin and vermouth is because the university president likes martinis too. We mainly just do beer and wine. In fact, I'm pretty sure I'm not allowed to sell you those martinis. I don't think we have the right liquor license for that."

"If you can't sell me the martinis, how am I supposed to pay for them?" Gwen asked. If she couldn't pay for the martinis, it would be incredibly hard to leave Etta an appropriate tip.

"We'll work something out." Etta made a dismissive motion with her hand. "I can offer you a beer. We've got some good, local craft beers. I'd avoid the wine entirely."

Gwen sighed deeply. "Something light, but not disgustingly so. Nothing domestic."

"Easy enough." Etta spun and pulled a can out of a below counter fridge. With a quick twist of her wrist, she popped the top. Then she grabbed a glass. With a quick look to make sure the glass was clean, she placed both in front of Gwen. "The brewery is eight miles up the road. They do interesting things with sours, but this is the regular lager."

"I'll take your word for it." Gwen poured the beer into the glass and waited for the foam to subside before taking a sip. She swallowed and pulled a face.

"Not your thing?" Etta asked.

"The only time I really like beer is when it's ninety-five degrees outside and I can't escape to the air conditioning." Gwen tried to take another sip, but she wrinkled up her nose as it hit the back of her tongue.

"I could have made you another martini. I've got just enough gin left to make one more." Etta looked like she was suppressing laughter.

"But then you couldn't have charged me for it. At least this way you're being compensated for your time." Gwen smiled at her.

"You know, if you don't mind waiting around, I can take you somewhere with a better drink selection." Etta's smile turned sly.

Gwen took it in and smiled back. "How late would I have to wait?" Gwen asked. She was certainly intrigued by the invitation. It wasn't every day that someone only slightly older than her son made a pass at her, and it certainly seemed like that was Etta's intent.

"We close at ten tonight. I'm normally out of here by ten fifteen." Etta replied.

"And where would we be going?" Gwen couldn't think of anywhere in town that might fit Etta's description, but it had been a while since she had lived there.

"That's a surprise." Etta challenged Gwen. "If you're brave enough."

Gwen looked at her watch. It was already after nine, which surprised her. She hadn't realized it had gotten quite that late. "I suppose I can be persuaded. If you promise me the drinks are worth it."

"They're worth it." Etta reassured her. Something about the way Etta said it made Gwen sit up straighter. Yes, this was intriguing.

Gwen made a snap decision. "Then I'll stay. And I'll have that last martini." Hopefully, her decision was the right one.

❖

"This is an apartment building," Gwen said as Etta turned the corner into the gravel parking area and carefully pulled into one of the few parking spaces. There was a larger, more stately home next door. This building looked like it might have been an outbuilding at one point in time, maybe a kitchen.

"So it is." Etta looked over at Gwen. "Is that a problem?"

Gwen looked back at Etta trying to judge the situation. She knew what was likely to happen if she went into Etta's apartment that night. Was that something she was interested in? "I was promised a drink."

"I think I've already proven that I can make you a drink," Etta murmured.

The breath caught in Gwen's throat and her heartbeat sped up. She was going to do it. She was going to say yes. "All right."

Etta looked at her with hooded eyes, then opened her car door, getting out of the car before Gwen had even thought about moving. She took a deep breath and opened her door to find Etta waiting for her outside of the car. It only took a few seconds to cross the parking area.

"The bar is just upstairs." Etta opened a door onto a staircase. "It's the door on the left."

Gwen nodded and headed up the staircase. She paused when she got to the top while Etta unlocked the door, stepped inside, and turned on a light before holding the door open for Gwen.

Gwen stepped into the apartment and looked around as best she could. They were standing in a small living room, which connected to a galley kitchen with bar seating. There was one door, which Gwen assumed led to the bedroom and bathroom. One wall was taken up by a modestly sized TV. The other wall had two deep-seated windows and a couch. There were books everywhere. Some of them looked like they were used on a regular basis. Others had knickknacks arranged on stacks of them. It was like Etta's entire decorating style was library chic.

"Give me your coat," Etta said from behind Gwen as she closed the door. Gwen immediately shrugged it off and turned to look at Etta as she handed it and her purse over. Etta took them both from her and put them on a coat rack behind the door. Then she put a hand on Gwen's waist and gently pressed her back against the door, using her own body to keep Gwen in place.

"I've been wanting to do this since I first saw you tonight," Etta said as she closed the miniscule gap that still existed between them. Gwen swallowed hard. "What? Pin me against your door?" This was getting real. Gwen hadn't slept with a woman since before she had married Christian's father, and they had been married for more than fifteen years before divorcing four years ago. Though she supposed that female anatomy hadn't really changed since then.

"Exactly." Etta brought a hand up to the side of Gwen's face and tilted it up just a bit before slotting their lips together. Gwen whimpered at the contact, then felt her cheeks go hot in a blush. It really had been too long since the last time someone had kissed her. It was embarrassing how turned on she was from something so simple. Her knees were trembling. She felt like she was going to vibrate out of her skin. She felt like she was going to fall over. She gripped Etta's suspenders for stability.

Etta kept moving her lips over Gwen's, and Gwen did her best to keep up. Etta braced her hands against the door on either side of Gwen's torso as Gwen brought her arms up to wrap around Etta's neck. Gwen opened her mouth and deepened the kiss. She was getting lost in the feeling of being wanted.

"You haven't had so many martinis that you're going to regret this in the morning, have you?"

Gwen could feel Etta's breath against her ear, and it made her want more. She was so far away from thinking about the morning, and right now, she felt like any regrets would be worth it. "Three drinks aren't enough to completely rob me of my senses." She found Etta's lips again and arched herself against Etta's front.

"Have you done this with a woman before?" Etta whispered. She looked at Gwen with intent. Part of Gwen appreciated the care, but most of her wanted Etta to get on with it.

"I'm not some coed you picked up at a club looking for adventure. I'm too old to be experimenting."

"Oh, I definitely think you're looking for an adventure, but I get what you're saying." Etta finally started to unbutton Gwen's shirt. She felt cool air against her cleavage where it spilled out above her lace-trimmed bra. She knew her skin was flushed. She tried to take a deep breath to steady herself, but it was robbed from her when Etta covered her breasts with her hands. It was all she could do to draw in quick, panting breaths as Etta kept touching her.

Etta moved her hands down to Gwen's stomach and then around her back. It took nothing more than a flick of the wrist to get Gwen's bra unfastened. If Gwen had thought she couldn't breathe before, when Etta's hands finally touched the skin of her breasts, she felt like she was going to pass out. It was ridiculous how quickly she had become overwhelmed. She would have been embarrassed if she had been at all capable of feeling anything other than desire.

Etta pulled lightly on her nipples and Gwen's legs almost gave out. Etta seemed to understand her problem right away.

"Let's find you someplace to lie down." Etta stepped away from Gwen, entwined their fingers, and led her through the single doorway to her bedroom. With the distance, Gwen finally felt like she could breathe again. She looked around the bedroom. It was small. A large daybed covered in too many pillows took up almost an entire wall, and Gwen wasn't exactly sure how they were both going to fit on it, but they would have to figure it out. It wasn't like either of them were interested in sleeping, after all.

Etta turned and smiled at her. There was something penetrating about it, and if Gwen didn't know it was absurd, she would think that Etta was looking deep under her skin, sussing out her every want and desire. It made her skin flush even more.

Etta tugged on their still entwined fingers and pulled Gwen close. "As hot as the unbuttoned shirt look is on you, it's time for it to go." She started to kiss her way down Gwen's neck as she untucked the shirt, then pushed it down Gwen's arms. It fell onto the bed. Right now, all she wanted was Etta, and Etta seemed completely on board with that. The morning would come when it came. Until then, she was going to enjoy herself.

Chapter Two

Etta didn't often pull all-nighters. She was too organized for that, getting her studying done at a reasonable time most nights, even if the rest of her life was often in chaos. The last time she had been up all night had been during the Bluebook exam she'd taken her first year of law school to get onto the school's law review. It had been worth it for the resume boost, but only barely. Now, as she looked down at Gwen, she thought that her latest all-nighter was more than worth the sacrifice. If you could even call it a sacrifice.

Gwen's eyes were closed, her light blond hair spread over Etta's pillow, but Etta didn't think she was sleeping deeply. She was probably just dozing a little as the sun came up. Etta skimmed her fingers down Gwen's forearm. She was too exhausted for any sort of more energetic activities, but she didn't want to stop touching Gwen. Presumably, Gwen would open her eyes soon and want to go back to her car.

Then they would never see each other again.

Etta might only be twenty-eight, but she knew how these things worked. This high-class, high-powered lawyer wouldn't want anything to do with the bartender turned law student the morning after. She'd gone into this knowing the outcome before they'd even started, but the thrill of it was too much to resist.

Gwen groaned lightly as she opened her eyes and Etta refocused on her.

"Hi there," Etta said as she looked down at Gwen.

"Mmm." Gwen blinked a few times. "What time is it?"

Etta fished around for her phone, miraculously finding it plugged in on her nightstand. She was amazed at her own thoughtfulness. She'd been so distracted last night, she was surprised it was even in the same room. A tap of the screen lit it up.

"Just before eight."

Gwen lifted her hands to her face and rubbed her eyes. "I should be getting back to Atlanta."

"I'll drive you back to your car. It's on campus, right?" Etta's offer was at least partially selfish. She'd take the extra ten minutes with Gwen before she disappeared from her life.

"It is. The real question is where are my clothes?" Gwen lifted her torso up off the bed, leaning on her elbows, as she looked around the room.

"Oh, they're here somewhere." Etta rolled out of bed, unselfconscious of her own nudity. She'd always been comfortable in her own skin. Being watched didn't change that. She pulled on a pair of leggings and a long-sleeved T-shirt, both of which she grabbed from the top of a pile on a nearby chair. Then she started looking for Gwen's clothing.

Her trousers were easy. They were pooled on the floor by the bed. Her bra and panties were next to them, but her shirt was nowhere to be seen. Gwen got out of bed, and as she did, her shirt fell onto the floor. Apparently, everything they did the night before had happened on top of Gwen's shirt.

Etta grabbed the shirt from the floor and held it up. The wrinkles were profound. "You should just borrow one of my shirts."

"I don't know that I have a choice." Gwen looked at her own shirt skeptically.

Etta laughed and opened a dresser drawer to pull a shirt out. The T-shirt was soft and black, with the law school's logo in dark green on the chest. It was something the school had given her at some point, and she didn't have any sort of emotional attachment to it. If Gwen never gave it back to her, she wouldn't miss it. She passed it to Gwen.

"Thank you." Gwen pulled the shirt over her head, then tucked it into her slacks. The contrast between Gwen's designer slacks and the free T-shirt made Etta smile. It was so incongruous. Etta wondered when Gwen had last worn a shirt that cost less than two hundred dollars. It couldn't have been any time recently.

"Back to campus?" Etta asked.

"Please." Gwen nodded.

❖

Gwen settled into the passenger seat of Etta's car. She took a deep breath, glad to know that she could properly breathe again after the excitement of the night before. She idly looked through her purse to find her phone. It was dead. She would have to charge it on her way back to the city.

"Everything okay?" Etta asked as she slid into the seat next to Gwen and pulled on her seat belt. She smiled over at Gwen before turning the key in the ignition. The engine turned over and Etta checked her mirrors before backing out of the parking space.

"Yes. Of course." Gwen swallowed and looked around. Part of her couldn't believe she had done it. She'd gone home with someone who was half her age, that she didn't know, and hooked up with her. It was absurd.

She'd only vaguely tried dating since the divorce, mainly with people Judith had set her up with, but everyone she'd had dinner or drinks or nights at the symphony with had been boring or overbearing or conceited. None of them had managed to talk their way into her bed. But five minutes with a bartender half her age had been enough to get her naked. She couldn't, she wouldn't, blame the martinis, and she didn't regret what she had done. She was simply baffled she had done it at all.

"I'm trying to reconcile what we did with how I normally act." Gwen gave a tight smile.

"Regrets?" Etta asked, concern plain on her face.

"No." She wanted to be clear about that. She did what she did because she had wanted to, and she hadn't been coerced. "I'm simply worried it might be the beginning of a midlife crisis, which I do not have time for right now."

Etta laughed. "You don't look old enough to be going through a midlife crisis."

"I appreciate the compliment, but I assure you, I am." Still, Gwen couldn't stop herself from smiling.

Etta smiled back. "I mean, it was just some fun, right? It doesn't have to mean anything."

"Of course." Gwen looked down at her hands. She was being ridiculous. Getting into a tizzy over the existential meaning of a one-night stand didn't suit her. She needed to stop.

Etta turned into the guest parking lot at the school and slowed down.

"It's the silver Mercedes down at the end." Gwen nodded in the car's direction.

"Clichéd much?" Etta asked.

Gwen knew she was being teased, but she didn't take offense. "It's classic," she merely said in return.

"If you're going to have a midlife crisis, you should really start with the car. Go buy something ridiculous like a Lamborghini or something," Etta said.

"I think I'll skip that part, thank you. I don't need to spend half a million dollars on a car to prove that I'm a man," Gwen replied.

"That's, wow, yeah. That's a lot of money for a car. I was thinking like two hundred K."

"You'd relegate me to a *used* Lamborghini?" Now Gwen was laughing.

"No, I suppose that would be completely unacceptable." Etta smiled. She coasted her car to a gentle stop behind Gwen's. "Here we are."

"So we are." Gwen unfastened her seat belt. "Thank you for the ride."

"Well, I couldn't leave you to the whims of Uber," Etta teased.

"I appreciate it." Gwen opened the door to Etta's car and got out as gracefully as she could wearing day-old pants and a too-big T-shirt. Etta waited long enough to see that Gwen got in her car before Gwen saw her raise a hand. Gwen waved back.

Settling back into the seat, Gwen started the car. She plugged her phone in and pulled on her seat belt. With a quiet buzz, her phone came back to life. She picked it up and looked at the screen to make sure she hadn't missed anything pressing. There was a phone call from Ben that she ignored. She would call him back after she got home. Then she saw a text from Christian. She tapped the message open. He had only sent it a few minutes ago, which was good, because it said he was at their favorite coffee place waiting on the breakfast she had promised him.

Panic welled up in Gwen's chest. She looked down at the shirt she was wearing and grimaced. There was no way she could show up to breakfast in someone else's clothes, but she didn't want to blow off her son either. Her ex-husband did that often enough that the thought of doing it as well wasn't acceptable. She took a deep breath. Both she and Christian would have to deal with her current mode of attire. Maybe he would think that it was one of Ben's shirts, even though there was no reason Ben would have one of the law school's shirts when he taught anthropology. It was flimsy, but it was the best she could do.

Rather than worrying about it anymore, she texted Christian that she was a few minutes away, then put her car in reverse.

Gwen finished parallel parking on the street outside of Cochran's Coffee and took a deep breath. It was like ripping a Band-Aid off, right? She looked down at her shirt one more time before opening her car door. Before she wanted to think about it, she was opening the door to the coffee shop and looking around for Christian.

His blond hair was easy to spot against the red brick wall he was sitting in front of. He looked strikingly like a young version of his father, handsome and a bit arrogant about it. She had done what she could to curb that arrogance when he was younger, but he was an adult now, and beyond her control.

He was facing the door, so it didn't take long for him to spot her. She watched as he did a double take, first looking past her and then focusing on her. He looked at her like she was a two-headed monkey for a second, then quickly schooled his features.

"I already ordered for us," Christian said as she stopped at his table. "I, um, got you the lox you like." He was still blinking too fast.

"Thank you." She smiled gently down at him, letting him have a moment to adjust to her unorthodox appearance. She pulled out a chair and sat down across from him. She was determined not to mention the shirt unless he did, and she hoped he wouldn't. The easiest way to ensure that didn't happen was to make him talk about something else entirely.

"So, how have you been? Is calculus still giving you fits?"

"Calculus is fine. I'm getting better at it," he said dismissively. Gwen knew that he never liked discussing his troubles, particularly not in public where someone might overhear them. Still, calculus gave plenty of people a hard time.

"All right." Awkward silence built between them. Gwen knew that the longer she let that go on, the more likely Christian would be to start asking questions she didn't want to answer. She floundered around for another question of her own.

"Are you seeing anyone?" She didn't want to turn this into an interrogation, but Christian didn't seem to be willing to say much, and she certainly wasn't going to talk about her night.

"I don't know. Are you seeing anyone?" His eyes flicked down to her shirt. It seemed she wasn't going to get out of this.

"I'm not currently dating anyone." Which was the truth. She and Etta had most assuredly not gone on a date.

"Ben told me that you didn't stay at his house last night. I went there to pick you up before I came here." Now Christian sounded petulant.

Damn it, what was she supposed to do with that? She didn't want to lie to Christian, but she certainly wasn't going to tell him what she had actually been up to.

"I stayed with a friend." She supposed she and Etta could very loosely be described as friends. "Ben was irritating me, so I found other accommodations."

Christian continued to look at her suspiciously. "You'd tell me if you got serious with anyone, right?"

"You'll be the first to know, I promise," Gwen reassured him.

"Now, tell me more about this situation where you *don't know* if you're dating someone." She arched her eyebrows. If he thought she had missed that detail, he had another think coming.

Christian deflated a little. "It's complicated. Too complicated to get into before I have to get to class. Can we just eat our bagels and not talk about it?"

"Of course," Gwen replied. She wasn't going to press him when she knew he had to leave in a few minutes. "I've got to get back to Atlanta anyway."

"Thanks." Christian smiled wanly.

Just then, the barista called his name.

"I'll be right back," he said as he got up to retrieve their coffee and food.

Gwen watched him walk the few steps to the counter where he picked everything up and headed back. It seemed like she had successfully gotten them past the subject of her shirt. They could finish their breakfast in peace, and then she would head back to the city. After all, she needed to go into the office that afternoon, and she'd have to go home and change before that happened. Wearing Etta's shirt to breakfast was one thing. Wearing it to work simply couldn't happen.

With the food in hand, Christian sat back down. It was nice to get to see her son before she had to go back. It wasn't something that happened often, so she was going to take advantage while she could. If he seemed more interested in eating than conversing, that was okay. She was still happy to see him.

❖

"So, how was your night?" Jorge draped his arm across Etta's shoulders. She had gone home after dropping Gwen off, long enough to shower and change into jeans, though she was wearing the same long-sleeved tee she had put on that morning. Her long, brown hair was still damp.

"No comment." She smiled up at him, leaning against his solid bulk. They'd been friends since halfway through their 1L year when she'd run into him in the waiting room of the school's mental health clinic. It had been comforting to know that someone else was getting worn down by the stress too. They'd bonded over that then, and now that they were most of the way through their second year, they had never been closer. He was her best law school friend, and sometimes they got to bartend together. Those were always good nights.

"That means something happened worth commenting on." He dropped his arm as they walked into the student lounge. Etta pulled her empty travel mug out of her bag and placed it under the single-serve coffee maker. No matter how enjoyable her night had been, it still meant she hadn't gotten any sleep. She knew she'd be dragging by midafternoon. Maybe she could fend that off if she started the coffee early. She put the pod in and pressed the button to make the machine start.

"I mean, yeah, something happened, but I'm not going to give you details." The coffee was dispensed into her mug, and she breathed in deeply. Even the smell was enough to perk her up a little.

"You sure?" He tried for a penetrating stare, one he might use on a recalcitrant witness, but Etta had seen him practicing it before their law skills trial, so now it only made her laugh.

"Positive." Etta poked him in the ribs to get him to move out of the way of the creamer and sugar. She put copious amounts of both into her coffee. During her 1L year, she had tried to drink her coffee black, but it had just given her heartburn. Now she was unashamed of how much her coffee didn't taste like coffee. "I need to go read my notes before Wills and Trusts. I don't want to sound like an idiot if Castaneda calls on me."

"You're, like, the smartest person here. You don't know how to sound like an idiot," Jorge replied.

"That's because I read my notes before class. Now, go bug your fiancée or something. I'm going to the library." Etta put the lid on her mug and slid past him into the hallway that would take her in the direction of the library.

"Fine. But if you end up marrying your one-night stand, you better ask me to be in the wedding." Jorge laughed at his own joke.

"Sure thing, buddy." Etta punched him lightly in the arm with her free hand. It wasn't going to happen. Not with Gwen. But having Jorge in her wedding was a foregone conclusion, just like she was going to be in his when he married Dominique. He and Dom were waiting until after they had both graduated and had taken the bar to plan the wedding, but Etta had no doubt the wedding would happen. They were crazy in love and would be for the next fifty years.

Just thinking about them made Etta happy. Combined with her night, it was easy for her to carry her smile into the library with her.

CHAPTER THREE

Gwen slid her car into a parking space outside the Granary in Buckhead. She didn't particularly like leaving Midtown if she could help it, but Grey had picked the brunch spot that month. She would need to drive down to Dunleavy Byrd after they ate to catch up on some work. Taking Friday morning off unexpectedly had set her back from her schedule. She had an appellate brief to edit that needed to be finished by Wednesday, and she already knew she'd be at work late both Monday and Tuesday night.

For the next two hours, however, she was going to enjoy brunch. Wind whipped up by the passing cars tangled her hair as she crossed the street. From there, it was a short walk to the Granary for brunch. Gwen opened the door and saw Grey waiting off to the side. The crush of people was almost overwhelming, but Gwen knew Grey would have made them a reservation.

She waved at Grey and then weaved her way through the crowd.

"Gwen!" Grey jumped up as she approached and pulled her into a hug. "I feel like I haven't seen you in forever." Grey squeezed her tighter.

"We have brunch every month. It hasn't been that long." Gwen laughed through Grey's complaints, though.

"But you canceled on me last month," they retorted.

"Wait. Wait, that's not how I remember it. You canceled on me." Gwen was willing to acknowledge that she had canceled on Grey probably too many times in the past, but she hadn't done it last month. Last month they had still been in the middle of the legislative session, and as the executive director of a lobbying group, Grey had barely had enough time to breathe, let alone eat. Things were winding down now, so they had agreed to resume their regular brunch meetings.

"Yes. Fine. But you were happy I did because you had oral arguments the next week that you needed to prep for, and you were going to cancel on me." Grey looked at Gwen pointedly.

"Okay. I surrender. Can we go to our table now?" The hostess was looking at them impatiently and Gwen didn't want to annoy her any more than she already had.

"Sure." Grey motioned for Gwen to precede them into the restaurant. They took their seats and waited for a server to approach their table. They had both been to the Granary several times, so they didn't need to look at the menu to order their mimosas or their breakfasts, and as soon as the server appeared, they did just that.

"So, how are preparations for the Gaydar annual gala going?" Gwen took a sip of her drink and relished the feeling of the bubbles popping on her tongue.

"You know I hate it when you call it that," Grey said.

"*You* called it that," Gwen retorted.

"That was before they put me in charge."

"Fine. How are the preparations for the LGBTQ+ Alliance Against Discrimination and Repression gala going?" Gwen shot Grey a look that made it clear she thought Grey was being ridiculous. People had started calling the lobbying organization Gaydar almost since its inception in the seventies as the Gay Alliance Against Discrimination and Repression. A simple rebranding in the nineties wasn't going to change that. Gwen thought they should just lean into the unofficial name, but ever since Grey had been made the executive director, they had insisted that Gwen use the group's real name. They thought it made the group sound more serious.

"Was that so hard?" Grey asked. "They're going good. As crazy as always when the end of the session overlaps with the start of gala prep, but we're making it work."

"Well, let me know when it's time for me to make my annual donation." Gwen had been donating to Gaydar for decades, even when David, her ex-husband, had questioned her loyalty to the organization.

"I will. Now, less talk about work. More gossip." Grey pointed at Gwen.

"You know I don't know any gossip. At least, not any gossip about anyone you know," Gwen replied.

"It isn't my fault you're a recluse. Don't you ever come down from that tower you live in?" Grey asked.

"I like my tower, thank you. And for your information, I spent Thursday night somewhere other than my tower. I had a board meeting down at T.R. and I ended up spending the night," Gwen replied.

"Spending the night with Ben doesn't count. I mean, he's less boring than you are, but that's not hard." Grey looked at Gwen with raised eyebrows.

"Ouch." Gwen reeled back. The teasing was nothing new though. "I'll have you know I did not spend it with Ben."

That made Grey sit up straighter. They leaned forward and placed their chin in one hand. "You didn't?"

Gwen looked around to make sure no one was listening to them, then realized how paranoid she was being. No one would be listening to the conversation between two random people at brunch. "I did."

"No. Way. I don't believe it. I refuse to believe it. If you don't give me details right now, I'm walking out and never talking to you again." Grey leaned back in their chair, but kept Gwen pinned with a look.

"Stop being so dramatic. It isn't entirely out of character for me to have a one-night stand," Gwen said.

"Except that it is. It absolutely is. Where did you meet? Tell me everything." Grey leaned forward in anticipation.

Gwen waved a hand, trying to look like she was more carefree than she felt. "We met at the on-campus bar. I went back to her apartment. I had a very nice night, and then I had breakfast with Christian in the morning and came home."

"And what type of person, pray tell, does one meet at an on-campus bar?" Grey narrowed their eyes before they suddenly went wide open. "You banged a student, didn't you?"

"Law student," Gwen rushed to clarify. "And how did you jump to that conclusion?"

"Please, if you'd spent your night with a professor, you would have come out and said so. Now, what's her name? What's she like? Are you going to see her again? Did you even get her phone number? You probably shouldn't call her, because kids these days don't like talking on the phone, but you could text her."

"Please don't remind me about how *kids these days* communicate. Besides, I didn't get her number. The only thing I got was her T-shirt." A small grin appeared on Gwen's lips.

"You wore a T-shirt? Like, a cotton blend T-shirt?" Grey looked at her in disbelief.

"I have no idea what sort of material it's made out of, and I have worn a T-shirt before. You, of all people, should know that," Gwen said.

"It's been a long time since we lived together as law students, and I doubt I've seen you in a T-shirt in the last ten years," Grey replied.

"Well, my shirt was too wrinkled to wear. And you're enjoying this far too much." Gwen waved a finger at Grey.

"I am absolutely enjoying this. You should be enjoying this." Grey pointed at Gwen.

"I enjoyed myself plenty Thursday night." That was an understatement.

"I bet you did. Now, when are you going back down there?" Grey asked.

"I'm not. Well, I am because I have to go to a committee meeting in a month, but I'm not going to see her again," Gwen replied.

"What do you mean you won't see her again? You have to give the shirt back. And then you have to see if she wants to go back to her apartment again. And you can't wait a month." Grey was emphatic.

"I'm not rushing back down there next week in hopes that she might want to have sex again. That would be pathetic." Gwen already felt a bit ridiculous. Having an affair with a twenty-something really would mark her descent into a midlife crisis.

"So, wait a week, concoct some legitimate reason to go down there, and just...swing by the bar while you're there. You need to return her shirt. If she's up for something, then great. If she isn't, well, then you won't have wasted a whole trip. Tell her you're there to see Christian or something."

"Christian is going to be suspicious if I suddenly start showing up to hover over him while he's at school." Gwen said.

"You don't actually have to see Christian. You can just tell her that when she asks why you're in town. Really, Gwen, you're smarter than this." Grey looked at Gwen like she was being deliberately obtuse.

"If I was so smart, I wouldn't have slept with her in the first place." Gwen ran a hand through her hair.

"Oh, no. No, that was definitely smart. Whatever impulse led you to do that, you should listen to it. You know you want to go back down there. I can tell. You're an adult. She's an adult, basically. You should have fun. Together." Grey's smile looked wicked.

"Why did I tell you about this? I shouldn't have told you about this." Gwen rubbed her forehead.

"Because you love me, and you know I thrive on good gossip." Grey looked pointedly at Gwen.

"You cannot tell anyone about this," Gwen said.

Grey looked skyward. "Of course I'm not going to tell anyone. I am, however, going to savor this knowledge. It will sustain me for at least the next two weeks. At which point you will have gone back down there and seen her again, and you'll have something new to tell me about." Grey took a sip of their water.

"I'm not making any promises," Gwen replied.

"Please. You can thank me later."

Gwen knew she was defeated. Grey wouldn't hear any more objections. She wouldn't go back to Cartersville. She wouldn't. She had more resolve than that. Grey would have to be disappointed.

❖

"You've finished the intake paperwork?" Etta asked the woman on the other side of the folding table. The Black trans woman fidgeted, and Etta could sympathize. The legal paperwork to change your name could be intimidating. It was even worse for changing your gender, and it had to be an entirely new experience for Tyesha.

"Yes, ma'am," Tyesha replied as Etta flipped through the pages to make sure that everything was done correctly. Etta felt weird being called ma'am, but she recognized that sometimes people fell back onto formality when they were in uncomfortable situations. Etta took care to use the name and pronouns that the person in front of her chose for themself, but she knew that the trans people who came to the clinic weren't always afforded that courtesy. Ma'am could be a defense mechanism.

"Nervous?" Etta tried to smile as reassuringly as she could.

"Yeah." Tyesha smiled back, though it was weak.

"I know it can be intimidating, but don't worry. The lawyers here have done a lot of these. We'll take care of you." Etta finished processing the paperwork and put it in a manila folder before handing it back to Tyesha. "You can sit in one of those chairs over there"—Etta nodded toward a small cluster of armchairs in the community center—"and someone will call your name as soon as they're finished with their current client."

"Thank you." Tyesha picked up her purse and carried it with her over to a chair.

This was the second year Etta had volunteered at the trans legal clinic that Gaydar was sponsoring in Cartersville. The legal clinic was Etta's way of contributing to the community and doing some pro bono work, and she didn't mind the additional stress that came from coordinating it. The lawyer who had done it previously had moved out of state when the Air Force stationed his husband in Oklahoma. Etta had volunteered to take it over. There was a bigger conference in the fall in Atlanta, and Etta was sure she'd be there too, doing the same thing.

Amy, another law student, popped her head through the door to the conference room where the clinic was taking place and called

Tyesha back. Etta gave Tyesha a thumbs up and Tyesha nodded at her.

A minute later, Grey came out of the room and sank into the chair opposite Etta on the other side of the table. "That's the last person, right?"

"That's the last person on my list." Etta looked down at her paperwork to make sure there weren't any other names on it.

Grey nodded and loosened their tie before unbuttoning the top button on their shirt. They closed their eyes for a moment before opening them back up again. They looked tired.

"I feel the same way." Etta relaxed back into her seat.

"It's been a long day." Grey twisted their head to the side to stretch out their neck.

"I'm so glad I'm not working tonight." Etta loved the clinic, and she liked her job, but she didn't know if she could do both on the same day. Jorge would be on his own that night, but he would be fine. Dom would probably show up and keep him company. Saturdays at the Bear's Den were actually pretty slow. Most of the students who were old enough to drink preferred to go off campus, and the ones who were too young knew that the law student bartenders were sticklers for having proper ID. "You're driving back to Atlanta tonight?"

"Yeah." Grey had their eyes closed in fatigue.

"You know you didn't have to drive down here. We would have had enough lawyers without you. The legislative session hasn't even finished yet," Etta pointed out.

"I know, but I like being able to get my hands dirty, so to speak. I almost never get to be a lawyer anymore. Let me have this," Grey implored, as if Etta had any say in the matter.

"Okay, okay." Etta laughed. "I won't kick you out. We do appreciate the extra set of hands."

"You're sure I can't tempt you with a summer internship?" Grey asked.

Etta looked down at her hands. She would be happy to work at Gaydar, but her bank account didn't agree. "I should hear something from Dunleavy Byrd next week. If I don't get it, I'd be happy to spend the summer working with you." She knew asking Grey to wait for her to hear something wasn't fair, and she hadn't exactly asked, but she knew Grey would hold the job for her if she wanted them to.

"They're going to offer you the job. You're beyond qualified, and you'll be a credit to them. It's just too bad that the alliance can't compete." Grey shook their head ruefully.

"Yeah." Etta rubbed her forehead. "You should head back to Atlanta. We can clean everything up here. There's no reason for you to get back even later than you will already."

Grey looked at Etta as if searching for a hidden message. Etta didn't know what they found. "You're sure?"

"I'm sure. Go home, Grey." Etta made a shooing motion with her hands.

"All right." Grey stood and gathered their things. "Hit me up after you move to Atlanta for the summer. I'll take you to lunch."

"I will." Etta stood up too and stretched. She walked Grey to the door and watched as they got into their car and drove away.

❖

Gwen pulled the T-shirt from the dryer and folded it up. She really did need to give it back to Etta. Etta hadn't said anything about her returning it, but it was only polite. She couldn't just keep someone else's clothing. She should wait until it was time for another committee meeting. Then she'd have a legitimate reason to be in Cartersville and wouldn't be grasping at straws for a reason to be in town when she saw Etta again. Assuming she even saw Etta again. She could go by the bar and Etta might not even be there. Gwen wasn't sure what she would do if that happened. She didn't want to seem like she was a stalker by going to the bar repeatedly.

Still, she did need to give the shirt back.

Thursday. She would go down on Thursday. She had met Etta on a Thursday, so it seemed logical that she would be bartending the next Thursday as well. Gwen would be finished working on the brief that they needed to file on Wednesday, so it would be fine if she showed up late for work on Friday. Hell, maybe she would take Friday off. She knew already that they'd be tweaking the brief up to the last minute before they needed to file it, which meant close to midnight. A normal person would take that Friday off. Sure, she'd never done it before, but there was a first time for everything. That was assuming everything went well and she wouldn't be driving back to Atlanta Thursday night.

Maybe she actually would take Christian to dinner that night. Then she could hear more about the person he might or might not be dating.

CHAPTER FOUR

G wen took a deep breath as she parked her car in the university's guest lot. Her heart was beating faster than normal, and she felt breathless despite her attempts to calm herself. It was ridiculous that this was making her nervous. She had argued cases before the Eleventh Circuit Court of Appeals. She had argued cases before the Georgia State Supreme Court. The only reason she hadn't argued something in front of SCOTUS was because she hadn't found the right case yet. Walking into a bar to talk to a law student should not be making her feel like this.

She had put the shirt in a small gift bag, not wanting to walk inside holding the evidence of her lapse in judgment. She'd almost added some festive tissue paper before she stopped herself. Even she realized that would be over the top. She was there to give the shirt back and that was the only reason she was there.

Still, she couldn't get Grey's voice out of her head. That voice was telling her to walk in and then see if Etta was willing to repeat their night together. Gwen actually had taken Christian to dinner that night, though he hadn't given her any real details about the person he might or might not be dating. He called it a situationship, a term that utterly baffled her, and refused to get into any details. In any event, it gave her a plausible reason for being in town. It wouldn't seem like she had come only to see Etta.

First, she had to get out of the car and go inside. For all she knew, Etta wouldn't be there, and all of this would have been pointless. Embarrassingly pointless.

Gwen opened her car door and stepped out of the car. She grabbed the bag, closed the door, and then headed inside. As she opened the door to the bar, she heard the same man singing Queen that she had heard the first time she had visited the bar. He hadn't gotten any better.

It only took a quick glance to find Etta behind the bar. Different shirt. Same suspenders and wristband halfway up her forearm. This time, she was wearing a terry cloth headband like she had been transported from the eighties. Gwen was certain Etta hadn't even been alive in the eighties. That thought almost gave Gwen pause.

Instead of stopping, she walked up to the bar.

The other bartender approached her. "What can I get you?" He was even bigger up close. Gwen barely came up to his shoulder and he had a look on his face like he knew exactly who she was and that he was going to give Etta shit about it later.

Gwen opened her mouth to request that he get Etta's attention for her, but he waved her off.

"Never mind. You're not here for a drink." He looked down the bar and called out, "Etta, you've got a visitor."

Etta looked over at him, a question forming on her lips before she made eye contact with Gwen. She tilted her head to the side in question before holding up one finger.

Gwen watched her pull a beer from the tap and place it in front of someone before she wiped her hands off on a towel and headed down the bar. The way she was grinning was almost insufferable, but somehow Gwen found it charming.

"Here for another martini? Because I hate to let you down, but someone came in and drank all of my gin last week. The manager was not pleased, and I'm not allowed to buy more." Etta's eyes glinted in the light, and she certainly didn't seem put out by drawing her manager's ire.

"Well, if you don't have gin, what good are you to me?" Gwen replied. She put the bag with Etta's shirt in it up on the bar.

"No good at all. Did you buy me a present?" Etta nodded toward the bag.

"It's your shirt." Gwen pushed it across the bar.

"Well, that's no fun." Etta picked the bag up and placed it on the backbar. "I was expecting at least a diamond tennis bracelet. I'd hate to think that I've left you with the impression that I'm a cheap date."

"Considering I didn't take you on a date, I don't know that you've left me with any impression at all," Gwen replied.

"And if that was true, you wouldn't be here revisiting a bar that is so far beneath your standards it might as well be in a basement," Etta said.

Gwen opened her mouth trying to come up with a suitable reply, but nothing came to mind. "You may have a point."

"Well, I wouldn't want to waste your time with pointless flirting. You're much too busy for that. Do you want to get out of here?" Etta nodded toward the exit.

"Don't you have a shift to finish?" Gwen felt like she was on the back foot, and she didn't know how that had happened. She hadn't felt this off balance in ages.

"Jorge can close up by himself. He's a big boy. He doesn't need my supervision. And it isn't so busy tonight that one person can't handle it. He'll appreciate the extra tips anyway," Etta said.

"Well, all right." The floor felt like it was shifting beneath her feet. How had they gotten to this so quickly? She had expected she'd have to be more coy, more circumspect. Instead, Etta had cut straight to the chase. Now she was coming around from behind the bar, the bag in one hand and a light jacket in the other. Gwen fell into step beside her as they walked out of the bar and into the student center.

"Do you want ride with me, or would you rather follow me home?" Etta asked.

"I can follow you. I remember where you live." They descended the short flight of stairs to the parking lot.

"Excellent."

Gwen stepped up to her car and was about to open the door when she felt a hand touch her wrist. She turned to Etta. Etta shifted them until Gwen was pressed up against the side of the car, then she leaned in for a kiss. Gwen felt the kiss deep inside as Etta's tongue brushed against her lips.

She was breathless as Etta pulled away.

She needed to pull it together. Crashing her car into a tree because she couldn't drive in a straight line was unacceptable. She needed to make it to Etta's apartment before she could fall apart.

Gwen briefly closed her eyes, then opened them again. Etta was smiling at her, and she looked like she was going to go for another kiss. Gwen flattened her hands against Etta's stomach and firmly pushed her away.

"We can do that at your apartment," she said.

"Okay. I'll see you again in a few minutes." Etta took a step backward, then turned around. Her car was only a few spots away, and she got in it, started it, and waited for Gwen to do the same.

Gwen ran a hand through her hair before she got into her own car. This was insane. She shouldn't be doing this. But there was something about Etta that was addictive, and she didn't know how to say no. She put her car into reverse and backed out of the parking space. Etta's apartment wasn't far enough away to give her time to come to her senses. She didn't even know if she wanted to come to her senses. Grey would be so proud of her.

❖

Etta didn't know what she was doing. She had never expected that she would ever see Gwen again, let alone that they'd go back to her apartment a second time. She hadn't expected that Gwen would seek her out. She'd never done this before, had a one-night stand turn into a two-night stand, but here she was, letting Gwen into her apartment to repeat what had happened a week earlier.

This wasn't a relationship. This was so far from a relationship. She didn't have time right now for a relationship. But it was certainly something. Apparently, she had left enough of an impression on Gwen that she had sought her out again. She didn't know if that spoke to her skill in bed, or something lacking in Gwen's life. Either way, she was going to enjoy herself that night.

"I never made you that drink I promised you," Etta said as she closed the door behind Gwen.

"I didn't drive an hour and a half to have a martini."

"Did you really drive down here just to see me?" Etta asked coyly.

"I drove down here to have dinner with my son. And to return your shirt." Gwen pursed her lips. She didn't appear to be amused. Etta ignored that. Gwen was standing in her apartment, after all.

"No, I think you came to see me, and I'm incredibly flattered." Etta reached for Gwen's hand and used it to tug her close. Their lips slid together, and Etta wrapped her arms around Gwen, holding her.

"You're being ridiculous," Gwen replied, but she didn't pull away.

"No, I'm not. And I'm sure you remember where my bed is." Etta kissed Gwen again before pushing her toward the bedroom. If she was going to do this, she was going to enjoy it. Wills and Trusts wasn't that hard anyway. She could afford to stay up all night.

❖

Gwen rubbed her eyes and yawned, shifting her legs against Etta's as she woke up. Morning light drifted into the room, and she felt a sense of déjà vu. This time she was in no rush to leave. She snaked her arm around Etta's stomach and pressed her face into the back of Etta's shoulder. She felt Etta twine their fingers together.

"Morning," Etta murmured.

"Mmm," Gwen replied. She placed an open-mouthed kiss on the skin in front of her.

Etta shifted in her arms and rolled over. "As much as I'd like to go with that thought, I have class at ten thirty. If we start, I won't want to stop, and then Professor Castaneda will wonder where I am. Then the next time she sees me, she'll ask if I'm feeling all right. And I'll have to come up with a suitable story for why I wasn't in class. She's really a very nice woman, and I don't want to have to lie to her. Plus, she tells really great stories, and I wouldn't want to miss another story about her ex-husband's great-grandmother who got buried alive and woke up when some grave robbers tried to steal her wedding ring."

"Wait, what?" Gwen blinked hard. Maybe she was still asleep? No, she couldn't have come up with something that outlandish in her dreams.

"True story. At least, as true as any other of Professor Castaneda's stories. The point is I can't miss class. I can take you to breakfast, though."

"You don't need to take me to breakfast," Gwen said.

"No, but I want to. And if I don't, you'll probably drive all the way back to Atlanta without eating anything. Or you'll go by Starbucks or McDonald's. I know a place that makes much better egg sandwiches than either of those places. Plus, they pay their employees a living wage." Etta was already rolling out of bed and hunting for something to wear.

"You've been arrested at a protest, haven't you?" Gwen narrowed her eyes in mock suspicion.

"No, but a girl can dream." Etta grabbed Gwen's clothing from where it was folded on Etta's dresser and handed it over. "Get dressed. I'm hungry. And I don't have to look in my fridge to know that I don't have anything edible in there."

Gwen laughed, but she did as she was told. Fifteen minutes later, they were stepping out of Etta's apartment and into the gravel parking lot.

"The place I'm thinking of is two blocks away. You can drive it if you want, but know that I'll be judging you as I walk." Etta started walking backward down the driveway, waiting on Gwen to catch up.

"I can walk two blocks, thank you. And if I couldn't, well, the car's electric." Gwen followed Etta onto the sidewalk.

"Really?" Etta looked at where Gwen's car was parked against the curb.

"I can be filthy rich and care about the planet at the same time.

Plus, it came with its own aromatherapy system, and who could turn that down?" Gwen kept walking even though she didn't exactly know where they were going.

"It has an aromatherapy system?" Etta was looking at the car like it had a jet engine and two wings instead of just four tires.

"It does," Gwen replied. "Though in full disclosure, I've never used it."

"Please tell me you give large amounts of money to charity, or I might never be able to look at myself in the mirror again." Etta sounded like she was kidding, but Gwen wasn't entirely sure.

"Am I too bourgeois for you?" Gwen smiled as she asked.

"Yes. Emphatically, yes. But I'll live in the hope that I can redeem you." Etta stopped in front of a storefront. Carter's Mercantile was written in script on the main window, and Etta opened the door and held it for Gwen.

"Every revolution needs to get funding from somewhere." Gwen stepped into the store and looked around. It was part corner grocery and part restaurant. There was a bulletin board covered in flyers next to the station filled with various milks and sweeteners. Gwen glanced at the flyers and saw one for an open mic night, another advertising a job at the local feminist bookstore. Gwen didn't recognize the name of the bar with the open mic night, but the bookstore had been around since the seventies.

Gwen reached out and lifted the flyer where she could read it better.

"Looking for a side hustle?" Etta nodded toward the flyer.

"No, but I remember hunting through the shelves for books about queer women's encounters with the legal system. It was the first year they offered a class on queer theory and the law, and the library hadn't quite caught up yet. There wasn't a lot of positive case law yet, so I was looking for memoirs. *Lawrence* didn't happen until the summer between my 2L and 3L years." Gwen let the flyer rest against the board once again. She turned toward the counter. "Now, you mentioned egg sandwiches?"

"Uh, yeah." Etta looked like she was considering something before she blinked it away and looked up at the board where the menu was written out in chalk. "Your choice of bread, protein, and cheese. I go for your standard bacon, egg, and cheddar, but if you want to try something more exotic, go for it. Their black bean sausage is excellent." With that, Etta stepped up to the counter and ordered her sandwich and drip coffee.

Without further examination of the menu, Gwen ordered the same thing. Before she could look through her purse to find a card to pay, Etta had already settled up.

"You didn't need to buy me breakfast."

"No, but I offered. I can't, like, buy a skyscraper like you can, but I can swing two breakfast sandwiches." Etta smiled a too charming smile and Gwen couldn't stop herself from returning it.

"I think either you've overestimated how much money I have, or you've underestimated the cost of real estate in the current market," Gwen replied.

Etta huffed. "Fine. No skyscrapers for you, but you take my point."

"I do. Thank you for breakfast." As Gwen said it, the cook pushed their sandwiches across the counter to them. They were wrapped in foil and accompanied by two cups of steaming coffee. They took their sandwiches to one of the small tables in the back before going over to the coffee station to make their drinks more palatable. Once that was finished, they settled at the table.

"So, this is where we awkwardly try to get to know each other, right? But not too much because we both want to be able to walk away." Etta's smile belied her words.

"I suppose it is. Why don't we start with you telling me what you want to do after you graduate?" That seemed safe enough.

"I'm not really sure. I've applied for a job for the summer at one of those ridiculous Big Law firms, but I'm not sure that's really where I want to be. I'll probably clerk for a year and then make a decision."

"State or federal?" Gwen didn't know what Etta's class rank was or how her GPA might stack up, but she certainly had the confidence to try applying anywhere.

"Well, I'm not getting a SCOTUS job. T.R. just isn't fancy

enough. But I was looking at the Eleventh Circuit Appeals Court. There are a couple of people there I could see working with."

"I can see your revolutionary bent doing well in McMillan's chambers." Gwen sipped her coffee, which was still a little too hot.

"Yeah, she'd be my top choice." Joyce McMillan was one of the most liberal judges on the East Coast. Etta would have to go to California to find someone more compatible with her beliefs. "You do appellate law, don't you?"

"What led you to that conclusion?" Gwen was fascinated by Etta's thought process.

"Most lawyers don't care about the political leanings of appeals court judges. They're too busy creating corporate documents or trying to put people in prison to spend time on who believes what, at least on any level lower than the U.S. Supreme Court." Etta took a bite of her sandwich.

"Well, you're right. I've just finished a brief for the Eleventh Circuit, which is why I get to take today off. We were at the office until after midnight on Wednesday making sure it was perfect before we filed it." Gwen had worked hard, and for once she was going to enjoy the time off that afforded her.

"That doesn't sound fun." Etta grimaced.

"I love my job. I love writing the perfect brief and then taking that brief and arguing it in front of the appeals court. I love convincing people that my interpretation of the law is the correct interpretation, even when they might not agree with me at first. It's hard. Don't get me wrong. And I've spent a lot of my life at the office until one a.m. making sure all of my i's are dotted and my t's are crossed. But it's been worth it," Gwen said.

"I hope I find something that makes me that happy."

"You don't think you'll be happy practicing law?" Gwen asked.

"It isn't that. I…" Etta looked down at the tabletop, then back up at Gwen. "I just haven't found my thing yet."

"You don't have to figure it out immediately. And you can always change your mind later." Gwen took a bite of her sandwich.

"Tell that to my mom." Etta slumped back in her chair. "She thinks I should go straight to Big Law and spend my life writing contracts and making money. I'm not, you know, entirely opposed to making enough money to live on, but I'd like to know that what I'm doing has had an impact on someone's life for the better. Where do you work?"

Gwen winced.

"Not something you feel comfortable sharing with your hook up?" Etta teased. "Afraid I might follow you to Atlanta and become a stalker?"

"Not precisely, I just..." Gwen trailed off. This needed to stay separate from her work life. This needed to stay contained.

"No worries. Pretend I never asked." Etta waved her off.

Gwen nodded. "Thank you." She looked at Etta intently, really taking her in under the light of day. "God, I'm old enough to be your mother, aren't I?" It was something she had been ignoring, but in this moment, she couldn't mentally brush it away.

"My mom is in her sixties," Etta pointed out.

"My son is nineteen," Gwen replied.

"And I'm twenty-eight. Significantly older than your son."

Gwen huffed. "Fine. I give up." Gwen never gave up on arguments she was truly invested in, but she was more than willing to be convinced in this case.

"Something tells me you don't say that often." Etta popped a piece of egg sandwich into her mouth and chewed.

"I won't invest effort into a losing argument. You are not quite young enough to be my child."

Etta beamed. "I appreciate you acknowledging my point." She balled up the foil that had been wrapped around her sandwich. "And I'm going to quit while I'm ahead. I need to get to school."

"Then I'll let you go. I wouldn't want you to miss learning the difference between revocable and irrevocable trusts." Gwen smiled as Etta stood.

Etta leaned down and kissed Gwen lightly before pressing closer and kissing her more thoroughly. "You taste like coffee."

"So do you." Gwen smiled even wider.

"Until next time." Etta shrugged as if she didn't know what else to say.

"Go to class." Gwen shooed her away.

With a wave thrown over her shoulder, Etta walked out.

Gwen leaned back in her seat and watched Etta pass in front of the window and back the way they had come. Would there be another time? She should probably stay in Atlanta. If it got out, hanging around a law student could put her reputation in danger.

Just as Gwen was finishing her coffee, the door opened up again, and Etta rushed in. She talked briefly to the guy taking orders. She scribbled something on his notepad and then turned back to Gwen. She held the piece of paper out.

"My phone number. Text me the next time you're in town." Etta flashed a smile as Gwen took the paper. Then she turned and hurried out of the store again.

Gwen looked down at the paper for a minute, then pulled out her phone to put the contact info in it. She opened her text messages.

She typed out *Let me know if you're ever in Atlanta* and hit send before she could think about it too hard. It was dumb. She knew it was dumb. She didn't care. She wanted to see Etta again.

Chapter Five

Etta was coming out of her negotiation class when her phone started buzzing. A quick glance at the screen showed her the name of the recruiter at Dunleavy Byrd she had been speaking with throughout her application process. She answered the call without taking the time to prepare herself.

"Ms. Monroe?" asked the caller.

Etta stepped out of the stream of traffic and held a hand up to her ear to block out the sound of the people around her talking.

"This is she." Etta's stomach started churning. She didn't know how this conversation was going to go. She didn't know how she wanted it to go. If she got the job, then she would be set for the next year. If she didn't, she could probably beg a job off Grey working for Gaydar for the summer. She still had time to apply for the public interest fellowship the school provided, though not much.

"This is Matt Hollins with Dunleavy Byrd."

"Mr. Hollins, it's good to hear from you again." Etta wanted him to cut to the chase.

"You as well. I called to extend an offer of summer employment to you. Dunleavy Byrd would be very pleased if you would accept our offer." Matt didn't sound particularly pleased. He sounded like he made this phone call a thousand times before breakfast. For all she knew, he probably did.

"That's…" Etta didn't exactly know what to say. She needed to accept, didn't she? She did. "Thank you. I'd love to spend the summer working there." Had she accepted too quickly? Was she supposed to tell him she'd call him back after she made up her mind? Well, it was too late for that now.

"Excellent. We'll send you an email with all of the details. If you need help with housing for the summer, we'll include the names of a few buildings that are willing to rent to our summer associates on a short-term basis."

"That's very thoughtful." Etta didn't want to seem ungrateful, though she was certain she could get a better deal finding an apartment on her own. She had a feeling none of the buildings the firm approved of came cheap. "I'll send back whatever paperwork you need to have filled out as soon as you send it to me."

She needed to call her mom and tell her the good news. Her mom, at least, would be utterly thrilled by this outcome.

"Sometime in the next forty-eight hours will be fine. I'll see you for orientation the third week in May. Have a good day."

"You too," Etta mumbled. Her brain was already going a mile a minute with everyone she needed to tell and everything she needed to do. By the time Matt had hung up, she was already figuring out what she needed to pack to survive a summer in Atlanta. She knew the firm did business casual unless there was a client meeting, but she would need shorts for the rest of the time. It was too hot in Atlanta to wear anything longer.

She would call her mom now because if she didn't, her mom would kill her, and then she would call Grey to tell them to stop holding that job for her. And then, well, Gwen had told her to get in touch if she was going to be in Atlanta. Maybe this summer wouldn't be so bad after all.

❖

Gwen stepped into the Atlanta offices of Gaydar and looked around. The offices hadn't changed since the last time she had been there. The wall behind the receptionist was painted in rainbow stripes, but the rest of the room was standard corporate functionality.

"Ms. Strickland, how can I help you today?" Queenie, the

receptionist, asked. Gwen didn't visit Gaydar often, but Queenie had a very good memory.

"Is Grey free? I have something personal I need to discuss with them, so I thought I'd drop by on the off chance they aren't in a meeting right now."

"Let me check." Queenie picked up the phone, and after a short conversation she turned back to Gwen. "They'll be out in a second."

Almost before she finished speaking, Grey appeared at the door that would lead them back to their office.

"Gwen, come on back." They waved Gwen through the door. "How are things? I didn't expect to see you before brunch next month."

Gwen smiled. "I have an idea I want to run by you."

They stepped into Grey's office, and Grey waved Gwen into a seat on a couch. They took the armchair next to it. "What's this idea that you couldn't email me about?"

"You saw the announcement that Carmichael is retiring?" Gwen leaned back into the couch. He had officially made the announcement the day before. It had gotten thirty seconds' worth of coverage on the local six o'clock news, but everyone in the legal community would know the significance of the announcement.

"I did. I'm hoping the governor doesn't replace him with someone who thinks just like he does. Though she's a lot more liberal than the guy who appointed Carmichael in the first place. Judgeships might be elected, but we both know that they're rarely contested once someone is in office. Why? Do you have some sort of inside track on who the commission is going to recommend? Is it an idiot? Are you coming to warn me?" Grey looked at Gwen in trepidation.

"No, I don't know who they're going to recommend. I have an idea about who I want them to recommend, though," Gwen replied, a coy look in her eyes.

Grey's eyes widened in terror. "It's not me, is it? Because you know I'd never want something like that. Really, it sounds like something you'd want."

Gwen saw the moment the lightbulb went off in Grey's head. "You want it to be you, don't you?" Grey smiled widely. "That's brilliant."

"I do." Gwen nodded. There was no use for false modesty with Grey.

"Amazing. This might be the best idea you've ever had. This deserves a drink or something."

"I'm not going to have a drink at eleven in the morning on a weekday. Besides, there's nothing to celebrate yet." Gwen tried to tamp down the feeling of excitement fizzing in her stomach. Nothing had happened yet. There was no reason to get carried away.

"Okay, you have a point. But we're getting champagne once you're appointed." Grey's smile somehow got even bigger. Then their face fell. "You know I can't say anything, right?"

"I know. The organization can't be seen to endorse a specific candidate. I'm not asking you to lobby on my behalf. I came because I wanted you to know personally. And because I want to know that I have your unofficial support."

"You know you do. Even though your firm poached away a promising law student." Grey wagged a finger at Gwen.

"And you know that I don't have anything to do with hiring decisions. Summer associates don't touch my cases." On that, Gwen was emphatic. Her cases weren't the place for summer associates to cut their teeth.

"I know, but I'm going to blame you anyway. Now, take me to lunch and tell me about your law student. Did you see her again?" They both stood up and prepared to leave the office.

"I returned her shirt." Gwen tried to keep a straight face.

"And?" Gwen knew Grey wouldn't let it go until she told them what was going on. She might as well fess up.

She looked at Grey from the corner of her eye. "And we ended up back at her apartment." She smiled a little at the memory.

"I knew it. I knew it. I mean, I'm not advocating that you marry her, but this is good for you." Grey clapped Gwen on the shoulder. "Better than a vacation."

"She gave me her phone number and told me to text her the

next time I was in town. Then, yesterday, she texted me to tell me she was going to be working in Atlanta over the summer."

"Are you going to see her again? Just so you know, there's only one right answer to that question." Grey looked at Gwen expectantly.

"I don't know. I'm not particularly good at compartmentalizing. At some point, it becomes more than sex, doesn't it? And she's twenty-eight. I'm not getting into a relationship with a twenty-eight-year-old."

"I'm not advocating for a relationship here. Just a summer of hot sex. You can compartmentalize that just fine. And if things get too intense, you break things off. It's simple." But then, Grey had never been much for serious, committed relationships.

"And if someone from the selection committee finds out I'm sleeping with a law student? That's not going to look great," Gwen pointed out.

"They're not going to find out. How would they find out?" Grey asked.

"I don't know. It feels like an unnecessary risk." Gwen couldn't stop herself from thinking about all of the things that could go wrong. It was simply in her nature.

"Your entire life has been decided by not doing the risky thing, and look where that's gotten you." Grey raised an eyebrow.

"I have a wonderful son and I'm a legitimate candidate to be named to the state supreme court. I'd say my life has worked out pretty well," Gwen replied.

"Yeah, but your life is boring. You have dinner with your sisters once a month. You have brunch with me once a month. You go to work. You go to the gym. You go to board meetings. Now that Christian is in college, you don't even go on vacations. Everything about your life is regimented. Nothing about that sounds fun. Go off and have some fun. No one is going to find out and you're not going to spontaneously develop feelings overnight." Grey made it seem so easy. And they made her life seem so dull.

"When you put it that way, I sound very boring," Gwen said. When had her life become so predictable?

"Exactly. Embrace not being boring for once. Tell your twenty-eight-year-old hookup that you'd love to see her again once she's in Atlanta. Your life will be better for it." Grey patted Gwen on the arm.

"I'll think about it," Gwen replied. She was already turning the idea over in her mind.

"That's all I ask." Grey smiled, as if they already knew what Gwen was going to do.

❖

Etta looked down at her phone and tried to decide if she wanted to send the text she had just drafted. She was going up to Atlanta on Saturday to look at apartments. Gwen had told her that she should let her know if she was going to be up there. That still didn't make the idea of texting her any less nerve wracking. It was just sex, right? She didn't need to stress about it. She'd just mention that she'd be in town and then tell Gwen when she thought she'd be finished for the day. Anything that happened after that would be up to Gwen.

She pressed send.

Then she put her phone away. There was no sense in staring at it until Gwen got back to her. It could be hours.

She startled when her phone buzzed only a few minutes later.

Pulling her phone out, Etta saw that Gwen had indeed texted her back. And invited her to dinner. That she was going to cook. At her condo.

Etta didn't know what to do. Should she say yes? She was incredibly curious about what Gwen's home looked like, but was she willing to get more entangled to fulfill that curiosity? It was only sex, wasn't it? Really good sex.

She called Jorge.

"Hey, where's the fire?" were the first words out of his mouth.

"No fire. Well, not a literal fire. But this is time sensitive," Etta said. Normally she would text him, but there was no telling when he might get back to her, and she needed some advice ASAP.

"I'm intrigued. What's up?" Jorge asked.

"Gwen, the woman from the bar," Etta started.

"You mean the hot blond you hooked up with? Twice," Jorge pointed out.

"Yeah, her. She lives up in Atlanta and I'm going up there to apartment hunt Saturday and I texted her about it and now she's invited me to dinner. Which she is going to cook. At her home. Her presumably very fancy home." Etta could hear the edge of panic in her own voice.

"And do you want to go to dinner at her very fancy home? And does dinner come with more amazing sex that you won't give me details about?" Jorge asked.

"Presumably, yes, it would involve more mind-blowingly good sex. But also, food. I mean, we had breakfast together the last time we saw each other, but that's different. I didn't cook the breakfast. It's, like, a whole other level of intimacy, isn't it?" Etta was normally able to be more decisive than this, but something about Gwen was throwing her off balance.

"I think it's whatever the two of you decide it is. If you want it to be a date or something, then that's what it is. If you want it to be a casual thing, then tell her that. Or say that you'd love to come bang her, but that you're not into the dinner part of the plans. Communication, man. It's all about communication. And breathing. You sound like you need to take a couple of breaths." Etta could tell Jorge was shaking his head at her.

Before she replied, Etta took his advice and inhaled deeply, slowly letting out the exhale. She felt a little better. "Right. You're right. Dinner only means what we want it to mean. Thank you for dropping everything to walk me through my crisis. You're a good friend, friend."

"I know. But don't tell Dom I'm so smart. I'm keeping it on the down low," Jorge said.

"I'm sorry, buddy, but Dom already knows," Etta replied.

"Damn. But you should stop talking to me and send an answer back to Gwen," Jorge said.

"Right." Etta exhaled again. "Right."

"I'll see you in class tomorrow."

"Yeah. Bye," Etta said into the phone.

"Later," Jorge replied.

Etta hung up the phone and flipped back to the screen with her text chain with Gwen. What did she want? Did she want to have dinner? She took Jorge's advice and took several more deep breaths before she started typing out her answer.

Gwen texted her back immediately.

It seemed like they were going to have dinner Saturday night.

Chapter Six

G rey, I've made a mistake," Gwen said before Grey could even say hello. She was sitting in her car in the grocery store parking lot, but she hadn't mustered up the courage to go inside yet.

"Okay," Grey responded placidly. "Is someone dead?"

"No." Gwen was on the verge of hyperventilating.

"Is someone going to prison for a long time because you screwed up their case?" It was an old fear from law school and part of the reason Gwen hadn't gone into criminal law. Grey bringing it up now actually wrested a smile from her.

"No. No one's going to prison." Gwen's breathing returned to something more measured.

"Okay, now that you can talk like a normal person, tell me what's going on," Grey said.

"I invited her to dinner. I offered to cook. I don't know what I'm doing, but it seemed like a better idea than possibly being seen with her and someone starting to ask questions." Gwen tried to keep her breathing steady, but it wasn't working well.

"Your law student?"

"Yes. Well, she's not *mine*, but yes." Gwen ran her fingers through her hair. She looked through the windshield of her car and watched the people coming and going from the grocery store.

"And presumably you spent an hour angsting about inviting her before you did that. I'm proud of you for figuring that one out yourself, by the way. So, what's the current problem?"

"I didn't spend an hour angsting. It was an impulse. And now I don't know what to cook." Saying it out loud made her sound ridiculous, but to their credit, Grey didn't laugh.

"Gwen, you've hosted literally hundreds of dinner parties in your life. You were practically born planning meals for people. You are an excellent cook. If I thought you'd give up the law, I'd hire you to be my personal chef."

Gwen sputtered out a laugh. "You couldn't afford me."

"That isn't the point. You are sublimating. This is not about what to cook for dinner. You realize that, right?"

"Yes. Of course, I realize that, but can we focus on the problem I can do something about and not the one I'm really freaking out about?" Gwen asked desperately.

At that, Grey did laugh. "Make the chicken with the balsamic reduction. It's delicious and you can do it in your sleep. Throw together a side salad and open a good pinot and you're set."

Gwen nearly collapsed in relief. "Thank you."

"Gwen, listen to me. It is going to be fine. You'll impress her with your cooking. You'll drink some wine. You'll end up in bed. And then she'll go home in the morning. You are not planning the rest of your life. It's one meal." Grey's advice certainly sounded reasonable.

"I know that. I do." Gwen turned her car off and prepared to get out. "Thank you."

"You're welcome. Have fun tonight. I'm hanging up now."

"Okay. I'll talk to you later." Gwen was smiling now and very glad that she had called Grey for their advice.

"Bye."

After hanging up, Gwen got out of her car and headed across the parking lot. Grey was right. She could cook a decent meal for two in her sleep. This would be fine.

❖

Etta waved to Grey as the restaurant door closed behind her. The sandwich shop had a good crowd and Etta stepped into line to order her food. It only took a moment before she was joining Grey at their table.

"So, are you ready to move to Atlanta?" Grey asked as soon as Etta sat down.

"I'm seeing two more apartments this afternoon. Hopefully, one of them will be worthwhile. I feel like my morning was a complete waste." Etta waved a hand, then let it fall to the tabletop.

"That's got to be annoying," Grey said sympathetically.

"Yeah, they were both at places the firm recommended, but from what I could tell, they were completely overpriced. I don't need a concierge or a doorman or a pool. I'm only going to be up here for a few months." Etta sank back into her chair.

"Yeah, you don't strike me as the concierge type." Grey looked up as a waitress placed their food in front of both of them.

"Yeah, no." Etta unrolled her napkin and started mixing the dressing into her salad. She stabbed the lettuce a bit too hard. "If those are the types of places Dunleavy Byrd thinks I should live, they're incredibly out of touch."

"You know, you could always rent a room from me for the summer. I've got the space," Grey offered.

"No offense, but I don't really do roommates anymore." Etta smiled to take the edge off her words. "I did roommates from college until I started law school, and now I've gotten used to living alone."

"No worries. I get the need for privacy." Grey picked up their sandwich and took a bite.

"Yeah. Hopefully, one of the places I see after lunch will be the one." Etta mixed her salad up a little more before finally settling in to eat it.

"I'll wish you luck, then." Grey nodded a little.

"Thanks." Etta really wanted to find someplace to live that afternoon. She wanted the problem settled. She didn't want to be stuck someplace at the last minute because she failed to find something within a reasonable time frame. She knew she could be picky about her living situation, but since she was dead set on living alone, at least she didn't have to take anyone else's feelings into account.

"So, Dunleavy Byrd for the summer, huh?" Grey asked.

"Yeah, we'll see what happens," Etta said. She still wasn't sure how she felt about the job, but it was done now. She had made a commitment, and she would see it through.

"You'll have a great summer. I'm still upset you won't be working with me this summer, but I suppose the alliance will survive without you." Grey smiled at Etta. "I know a few people who work there. Once you get settled, I'll set up some lunches or something. I know at least one of them doesn't let the summer associates work on her cases, so you might not meet her otherwise."

"I'd appreciate that." Etta didn't really know what else to say to the offer. It was nice of Grey, but she wasn't sure she wanted to spend ten weeks at networking lunches. Still, she guessed it came with the territory. And if these people knew Grey well enough to have lunch with them, then maybe the lunches wouldn't be so bad.

"So, do you know anyone else in Atlanta?" Grey asked.

Etta blushed. Did Gwen count as knowing someone? "Not really."

"Your face is awfully red for someone who doesn't know anyone," Grey teased and Etta wondered just how much they could figure out based on that alone.

"I, uh…" Etta didn't know what to say. Grey wasn't really someone she shared that aspect of her private life with.

"It's fine. You don't have to tell me." Grey held their hands up. "But I'm glad you're having fun. This could be a very long summer for you if you spend every waking moment with people from the firm."

Etta smiled slightly. "Yeah. I'll be fine."

For now, Etta was going to focus on apartment hunting and then she was having dinner at Gwen's. She had more than enough to worry about without stressing about the summer yet.

❖

It was six thirty-five and Gwen was getting antsy. Etta had agreed to come over at six thirty and she was late. It was probably because of some unexpected traffic. Even on the weekends traffic in Atlanta could be atrocious. Still, she couldn't help but think that Etta had changed her mind and decided not to come.

She had just picked up her phone to check her texts when it started ringing. It was the front desk. She answered and confirmed that she was expecting a guest before hanging up. The elevator would take a minute, so she looked around her kitchen one more time. The chicken was nearly finished. The salad was in a bowl. The wine was open.

She finished her survey just as Etta knocked on the door. Gwen strode across the condo to open it and smiled as Etta came into view.

"Welcome." Gwen stepped back and allowed Etta inside. There was a moment where Etta looked uncertain, but the look quickly left her face.

"Thanks." Etta walked in and then turned to wait for Gwen to catch up with her. She held out a small gift bag, which Gwen took from her. "It's a candle. I know it's—" Etta shrugged. "I panicked. I mean, I didn't want to try to buy wine and then my mind went blank. I sorta bought it in a fugue state in Target."

Gwen laughed. "Thank you. I'm sure it's lovely." She put the gift bag down on a side table. "Give me five more minutes and dinner will be finished. You can have a seat out here or you can follow me into the kitchen."

There wasn't much of a difference between the living room and the kitchen in the open plan condo, but Etta followed Gwen to the kitchen area.

"I've got a light red open, but if you want to switch to white, we can do that. Assuming you even like wine?"

"I do. And red is fine." Etta rested her hands on the edge of the kitchen island. Gwen watched as Etta flexed them nervously.

"Hey," Gwen said as she covered one of Etta's hands with her own.

Etta looked startled. Gwen realized Etta was probably more nervous than she was. After all, she wasn't standing in someone's home trying to figure out how to be polite in this slightly weird situation. Gwen picked Etta's hand up and squeezed it lightly before guiding it up and around her neck. Etta seemed to get the hint and brought her other arm up to wrap around Gwen's neck. Then Gwen leaned in and pressed her lips to Etta's. The kiss built slowly, but as it did, Etta seemed to relax.

They knew how to relate to each other this way. Their entire relationship was based on the physical. Going back to that put both of them more at ease.

The kiss slowly wound down, and as Etta opened her eyes, a smile tugged at her lips.

"Better?" Gwen asked.

"Yeah." With newfound confidence, Etta scratched her nails against the nape of Gwen's neck and maneuvered them around until she could press Gwen up against the counter. Etta brought their lips back together.

Gwen was happy to sink into the kisses. The food would hold for a few minutes.

Eventually, the kisses came to an end. When she came back to herself, Gwen realized she was halfway to climbing onto the counter where she could wrap her legs around Etta. She pushed Etta away slightly, just enough to give herself some breathing room.

"Did you still want to have dinner? Or should we forget about eating and start making out on the couch?" Gwen asked.

"Well, I was looking forward to finding out if you can cook." Etta finally smiled. "And lunch was a long time ago."

"You'll have to let me go if you want me to feed you."

Etta huffed and took a step backward. "Fine. I suppose I can do that."

"Thank you." Gwen quickly kissed Etta before sliding away from her. The first thing she did was pour Etta a glass of wine and hand it over to her.

Etta took a deep breath to smell it before she took a sip. "How did I know you'd have really good taste in wine?" She took a second sip.

"I like to think I have good taste in many things." Gwen gave Etta a significant look.

"Are you implying I'm one of those things? Are you flirting with me?" Etta batted her eyelashes in an overexaggerated way.

"That was, in fact, what I was trying to imply. Though it's been a while since I've flirted with anyone, so I might not remember how to do it."

Gwen grabbed a potholder and pulled the chicken out of the oven, then placed it on the stove.

"How long has it been since you flirted with someone?" Etta asked.

"I don't know if that's a particularly polite question," Gwen replied with a smile. "But my divorce was finalized three years ago, and I was married for seventeen before that. And I'll be forty-five next February. That's what you really wanted to know, wasn't it?"

Etta blushed. "That's the information I was angling for, yes. What's your son's name? I know you said he was nineteen."

Gwen turned to the refrigerator and pulled out the salad. "Christian. His father chose it."

"Not a fan?" Etta asked.

"I'm a fan of my son," Gwen said.

"A diplomatic answer," Etta replied.

"I lost a bet." Gwen didn't like admitting that, but it was the truth.

"What?" Etta asked.

"David and I had a bet who would replace Rehnquist on the Supreme Court. It was an incredibly stupid thing to bet on, but he won." Gwen started putting the salad in two bowls.

"So, you let him name your child because John Roberts is chief justice now?" Etta looked at her incredulously.

"I did. We were always doing things like that, betting on the most ridiculous things. Normally the terms weren't quite so weighty, though I did get him to marry me by having a better GPA than him at the end of my 2L year," Gwen said ruefully.

"He didn't want to get married?" Etta asked before taking another sip of her wine.

"I..." Gwen stopped and pushed the salad away. "I wouldn't

say that." She thought hard about what she wanted to tell Etta about her previous relationship before she started speaking again. "We disagreed about the timing. He wanted to wait a few years after graduation. I thought waiting was pointless. And I thought that my career would recover faster if I had any children early rather than taking time off when I was in my late twenties or thirties. It was more pragmatic than it was romantic, though from a pragmatic perspective, trying to plan a wedding while studying for the bar was not the best decision I ever made."

"Do you mind if I ask what happened?" Etta put her wine glass down and looked at Gwen intently.

"Oh, nothing really happened." Gwen reached for her own glass of wine and took a slightly too big sip. "One day he just told me he didn't love me anymore. He never particularly explained what that meant or what convinced him that we shouldn't stay married. I was—"

Gwen tried to push away the emotions that the discussion had brought forward. This wasn't a conversational topic she had anticipated. "I was completely blindsided." She looked into the middle distance. "He remarried nine months after everything was finalized. According to Christian, they're wildly happy together."

"Do you think he was cheating on you?" Etta's eyes went wide as soon as she asked the question. "You don't have to answer that. I should not have asked that."

Gwen waved a hand. "I have my suspicions, but I don't really want to know. It's his conscience, not mine."

"I guess that's a healthy way to think about it." A look of mischievousness came into Etta's eyes. "Besides, now you get to have hot revenge sex with someone half your age."

"If that's true, I've waited a very long time to get my revenge." Gwen turned and picked up the now full salad bowls and carried them over to the table.

"Well, I don't mind being your hot, young revenge hookup." Etta grabbed the two plates of chicken and followed Gwen.

"I hope that means you're up for my planned debauchery later." Gwen flashed a smile.

"I can do debauchery." Etta slid into a seat that had an exceptionally good view of the Atlanta skyline.

Gwen went back to the kitchen to grab their glasses of wine, and after she dropped them off, she took her own seat. She was glad that they had moved on from the depressing story of her divorce and had found their way back to the light flirting that had marked their relationship so far. She wasn't with Etta because she wanted someone to bare her soul to. She was with her because the sex was good and spending time with her was fun.

❖

Etta gasped for air and arched up from the bed. Her hands scrabbled against the sheets looking for purchase. Gwen's tongue slid against her clit and Etta could barely contain herself. She curled her toes and pressed one of her heels down into the mattress. She was pretty sure Gwen had been between her legs for an hour, though it couldn't possibly have been that long. Still, it felt like it was never going to end. A great shudder coursed through her entire body, raising goose bumps on her sweat-beaded skin. She had already had one orgasm that night. It seemed like Gwen was determined to bring her to another.

Before they'd had sex the first time, Etta was convinced that Gwen really was only looking for an experiment, even if she had said that she wasn't. Forty-something bisexual sex goddesses didn't just walk into your life and agree to go to bed with you with almost no leadup. Etta had figured she'd be the one doing all of the work, and she had been willing to do it. Gwen was hot enough to make her brain melt a little just from looking at her. If Gwen had gotten off and then fallen asleep, Etta wouldn't have been disappointed, but she also wouldn't have repeated the encounter.

Instead, she had found that Gwen was more than willing to get her hands dirty, and she had a mouth worth killing over.

Etta moaned as Gwen touched a particularly sensitive spot.

With a seductive smile on her face, Gwen lifted her head from between Etta's legs. "How do you feel about toys?"

"Sex toys? Or are we talking LEGOs? Because I like both." Etta panted out an answer.

Gwen laughed. "I was thinking sex toys, but I'll keep your love of LEGOs in mind for the future."

"Were you thinking something specific, or was it a hypothetical question?" Etta was slowly catching her breath.

"I bought a strap-on when you told me you'd be in Atlanta for the summer. I'm hoping I didn't get ahead of myself." Gwen scratched her fingers against the skin of Etta's outer thighs.

"Oh, God." Just the thought of Gwen with a strap-on was enough to completely derail Etta's brain. "If you don't fuck me, I might die."

"Well, we wouldn't want that." Gwen pressed a kiss to Etta's inner thigh before sliding out from between her legs. "I'll be right back."

Gwen got out of bed and disappeared into what Etta assumed was a huge walk-in closet. Etta watched her go and tried to restart her brain. She knew she wouldn't have long before Gwen came back out and then all of her faculties would be shot. She took a long, deep breath and tried to prepare herself.

It was pointless, though. As soon as Gwen stepped through the door, Etta's brain went blank. The harness was black leather, the dildo was purple, and Etta wanted it inside her right now.

"Christ," Etta said as Gwen stepped closer.

"Too much?" Gwen asked, but she stood so confidently that she obviously knew the answer was no.

"Seriously, get over here and fuck me. It's vital to my continued health because looking at you like that is going to give me a heart attack." Etta shifted her legs and squirmed.

Gwen tossed a bottle of lube on the bed.

"I don't think you're going to need that," Etta said as she grabbed for the bottle. Gwen plucked it out of Etta's hand and leaned down to kiss her.

"I'm going to use it anyway." Gwen popped the top, squeezed out some of the lube, and coated the dildo with it.

"Holy fuck that's hot." Etta squirmed again and reached for Gwen.

Gwen slid easily into Etta's arms and shifted until she was between Etta's legs. "Are you ready?"

Etta wrapped her legs around Gwen's hips. "If you're looking for my consent, you have it. Now, fuck me." Not content to wait around for Gwen to start the show, Etta reached between Gwen's legs and started to guide the dildo into herself.

Gwen allowed herself to be guided and Etta groaned as the dildo slid all the way inside her. Gwen held herself still while Etta got used to the feeling. It didn't take her long. Etta flexed her hips and started moving against Gwen.

With all of her attention focused on the area between her legs, Etta was taken by surprise when Gwen started kissing up the length of her neck until she reached a sensitive place behind her earlobe. Etta stuttered in her movement and wrapped her arms around Gwen to pull her closer.

They rocked together, each thrust of Gwen's body against hers brought Etta closer to the edge and made her mind fuzzier. She gasped as Gwen angled her hips and started to rub the dildo against the perfect place inside her. She couldn't keep her eyes open, and colors started to swirl behind her eyelids. She could feel Gwen's breasts pressed against her own, and she couldn't get close enough.

"Touch your clit," Gwen whispered into Etta's ear, and it was almost enough to make Etta come from that alone.

Etta let go of Gwen with one arm and did as she was told. As soon as she touched her clit, her eyes snapped open and then closed again. She groaned deeply and started rubbing her clit in the way she knew would bring her over the edge. Gwen started to push into her with more authority, and almost before she was ready, her vision went white then black as her orgasm overwhelmed her. She flexed her legs to pull Gwen as close as she could while she rode the dildo through her orgasm.

With a sigh, Etta felt all of her muscles relax and go limp. She whimpered as Gwen slowly pulled the dildo out of her and came to rest beside her. Etta rolled onto her side to wrap an arm around Gwen's waist. She weakly pushed Gwen onto her back and curled up against her.

"Are you all right?" Gwen whispered.

"Mmm," was all Etta could manage. She placed a kiss on Gwen's neck.

Gwen laughed. She reached down to unfasten the straps of the strap-on, but Etta put her hand on top of Gwen's to stop her.

"I'm not finished with you yet." She took a deep breath. "Just give me a few minutes."

Etta closed her eyes and started trying to breathe normally again.

❖

Gwen stroked a hand down Etta's spine and smiled as that made Etta press even closer to her. With a great, shuddering breath, Etta levered herself up onto her knees.

Gwen couldn't believe that she was having the best sex of her life at the age of forty-four. A month ago, she would have said that was behind her, left somewhere in her twenties. She was so, so wrong. She stared up at Etta, amazed that someone as young and attractive as Etta would even want to go to bed with her. Yet here they were.

Etta leaned over Gwen and swiped her tongue over one of Gwen's nipples. Gwen gasped at the quick contact. She reached for Etta only for Etta to evade her grasp and capture her hands. Etta pressed her hands down onto the bed and slid them up over her head. With a bit of extra pressure, she said, "Stay." And then let go.

Gwen wasn't accustomed to being told what to do in bed, but the rush that went through her at the words left her more than willing to obey. She shifted slightly to make herself more comfortable but left her hands in place.

Etta rolled back onto her knees and stared down at Gwen. She reached between Gwen's legs and touched the dildo for a moment before she slid down Gwen's body and came to rest between Gwen's thighs.

"Let me know if this doesn't do anything for you." It was the only warning she got before Etta ducked her head down and licked a stripe up the underside of the dildo. She took the tip into her mouth, and even though Gwen couldn't feel it, the visual was enough to make her groan and curl her toes. She pressed her arms down into the bed to stop herself from reaching for Etta. If Etta wanted her to keep her hands to herself while she went down on her, then she would.

Etta stopped sucking for a moment and said, "I guess that answers that question," before she moved to take the dildo back into her mouth. She wrapped one hand around the base and pressed the dildo back against Gwen.

It wouldn't provide enough friction against her clit to get her off, but Gwen didn't care. Watching Etta was making her so wet that she was sure that as soon as Etta touched her clit, she would orgasm within seconds. Gwen had never received a blow job before, but Etta certainly looked like she knew what she was doing. Knowing that Etta was tasting herself on the dildo only made the experience more overwhelming.

Etta moaned as she took the dildo further into her mouth. Gwen shivered. She flexed her hands against the bed one more time.

"Touch me. God, please touch me," she begged.

She could see Etta's satisfaction. It only made her more turned on. She felt the straps around her hips loosening, then suddenly the strap-on was gone.

"I'll do whatever you want when you sound like that," Etta said, before she ducked her head back down to take Gwen's clit between her lips.

Gwen shouted at the touch and arched up into Etta's mouth. Her brain barely had time to catch up to the new sensation before she crashed into her orgasm. She gasped and sucked in a breath as Etta kept licking her. Finally, Etta slowed down and pulled away. She crawled up Gwen's body and settled against her.

"You can move your hands now," Etta said with a teasing smile. Gwen groaned and brought her arms down and around Etta.

"I'm surprised you kept them up there for so long." Etta pressed her face against Gwen's neck.

"I didn't want you to stop." Gwen knew she still had a blissed-out look on her face.

Etta lifted her head off Gwen's shoulder and looked down at her curiously. "If I told you to do other things, would you do them?"

Gwen thought about it for a minute, but it was hard to get her mind to function properly. "I think it would depend on what it was."

"Mmm." Etta laid her head back down on Gwen's shoulder. "We should talk about that when we're both not swimming in oxytocin." She placed a hand on Gwen's stomach.

"If that's something you want." Gwen nuzzled against Etta's hair as her eyes started to close. Talking about what they both liked during sex was admitting that they would be doing this again, maybe all summer. It wouldn't be just the occasional hookup. The thought should have scared Gwen, but she was feeling too relaxed for that. She didn't have anything pressing to do the next day. Maybe they could do this again when they woke up. She tangled her legs with Etta's and let sleep take her.

Chapter Seven

T he nominating commission is officially soliciting expressions of interest for the supreme court vacancy," Grey said without preamble as soon as the phone call connected.

"Yes, I know."

"So, have you sent one?" Grey asked with an urgency that Gwen didn't feel yet.

"I have a few days. I'm prepping for oral arguments right now. And I still need to tell the firm's managing director that I'm going to be applying." Gwen wasn't particularly looking forward to that conversation. She didn't think that Brad would react badly, but once she told someone outside of her circle of friends and family, it would become real. It would be hard to take back.

"He's going to be thrilled to have someone from the firm on the supreme court. And if you don't get appointed, you're staying at the firm, right? There are no downsides for him."

"There are if I embarrass myself." Gwen spun around in her chair to look out her office windows.

"Gwen, you are the leading appellate litigator at Dunleavy Byrd. Hell, you're probably the best one in the state, if not the whole Eleventh Circuit. You've never faced a malpractice claim in your career. You are ethically unimpeachable. I don't want to hear this imposter syndrome bullshit. You will not embarrass the firm. You will not embarrass yourself. Write the damned letter to the commission," Grey said emphatically.

"Are you finished?" Gwen asked, though she did feel better after Grey's speech.

"Yes. But I can keep going if you need me to," Grey replied.

"No, I think you've done a good enough job as a cheerleader. I'll write the damned letter as soon as we get off the phone. And I'll go see Brad as soon as he has a free moment." Gwen was smiling now.

"Good. Now, I know it hasn't been a month yet, but I demand you have brunch with me this weekend. I need an update on your sex life," Grey said.

"You know, we can find you a sex life and then you can stop obsessing over mine." Gwen leaned back in her desk chair.

"My sex life changes every two weeks. You know that. By my count, you've seen your law student at least three times now over the course of six weeks, and before that, you were a hermit. That development is much more interesting. Brunch Sunday. If you don't show up at the Granary on time, I'll come by your place and kidnap you."

"All right. Fine. I'll see you Sunday. Now go back to work."

"Yes, ma'am," Grey said before they hung up.

Alone again, Gwen turned back around and opened a new document on her computer. Grey was right. There was no sense in waiting to write her interest letter. Her oral arguments could wait for the hour it would take to draft the letter and speak to Brad.

❖

"Hey, Gwen, come on in." Brad waved Gwen through the door into his office and past his administrative assistant. "Take a seat." He directed her toward the sitting area off to the side of his office.

Gwen settled into an armchair. She had a leather folio in one hand.

"You were pretty vague about why you wanted to talk to me. What's up?" Brad looked at her curiously.

"I think you should read this." Gwen opened the folio and produced a piece of paper that she handed over to Brad.

"You're not resigning, are you?" There was a hint of panic in Brad's eyes as he sat down.

"Not exactly." She nodded toward the paper.

Brad started reading, his brow furrowed. Slowly, he started to raise his eyebrows until finally, he looked up at her. "You want a supreme court seat?"

"I do." Gwen nodded.

"That's…" Brad paused and looked at her more closely. "The firm is going to be very sad to see you go."

"I haven't been appointed yet," Gwen replied. To the extent that she had felt nervous talking to Brad, that nervousness abated.

"But you will be. I have complete faith that you'll be the most qualified candidate. The governor won't have a choice." Brad seemed fully confident that she would get the job.

"The governor always has a choice. She could completely disregard the commission's recommendations." Gwen couldn't stop herself from pointing out the obstacles to her appointment. She didn't want to get her hopes up too high.

"She won't. And then I'll have to find a way to replace you. You've been a credit to this firm, Gwen, and you'll be a credit to the state of Georgia once you take the bench. To whatever extent you need my approval, you have it. And when you have to run for election in a year to keep your seat, you'll have my vote." Brad stood up and offered Gwen his hand.

With a deep breath, Gwen stood up as well and took Brad's hand in a firm handshake. "Thank you."

Brad walked Gwen to the door of his office and then stopped. "I expect an invite to the celebratory party you have once you've been appointed."

"You'll get one." Gwen smiled confidently before leaving Brad's office and heading back to her own. She had a letter to mail.

❖

"So?" Grey asked as Gwen sat down across from them.

"So what?" Gwen knew what Grey wanted to talk about, but

she couldn't help but string them along a little bit. It was more fun this way.

"Well, two things, actually, now that you mention it." Grey took a sip of their mimosa. "One, did you send that letter? Two, what's going on with the law student?"

"Yes, I sent the letter." Gwen ran a hand through her hair. "I sent the letter the day we talked about me sending the letter."

"Good," Grey said. They reached for Gwen's hand. "You really are incredibly qualified. If you felt like waiting, you could probably get a federal judgeship one day."

"There's no way to know that. At least with the state court, I have some measure of control." Gwen had thought hard about what she wanted. A judgeship at the federal level was an interesting prospect, but it was impossible to predict when or even if she might get appointed. The Georgia State Supreme Court was right in front of her, taunting her to reach out and take it.

"You'll make an excellent judge no matter where you end up." Grey smiled. "Now, tell me about your law student."

"Once again, she isn't my law student. She's her own person. But things are going well. Once I finished freaking out about dinner, we actually had a good time. Or at least I did." Gwen smiled back at Grey. Then she looked away. "I might have told her the story of my divorce. I'm not sure I should have done that."

"Do you think it's going to run her off or something?" Grey asked.

"I think it might turn something that's supposed to just be sex into something else." Gwen furrowed her brow and fidgeted with her napkin.

"Gwen, you absolutely cannot get into a relationship with her. You know I support your sexcapades, but you need to remember she's half your age. That way lies disaster."

"She's sixteen years younger than me, which is not half of my age." Gwen couldn't stop herself from presenting a compelling argument. Arguing was in her blood.

"The fact that you are trying to justify this to me does not bode well for you keeping this thing impersonal," Grey replied.

The conversation stopped while the server delivered their food. Grey picked up her fork and pointed it at Gwen. "Seriously, you need to disconnect a little."

"You're probably right. I told you I was bad at compartmentalizing," Gwen said.

"You need to figure it out, or you need to stop seeing her. The sex might be fantastic, but she isn't worth potentially derailing your bid for the supreme court if it comes out you're dating a law student. She's a summer fling. Make sure she stays that way." Grey sounded emphatic, and they were right. Gwen needed to step back.

Etta had exams soon. Maybe that was the right time to pull back. Etta would be too busy to notice that Gwen wasn't talking to her as much.

"I already told you you're right. It isn't a relationship, and it isn't going to become one." Gwen picked up her own fork and cut into her omelet. She and Etta weren't in a relationship. She could do this.

❖

Etta hit print on the last of her final exams for the semester. She watched as the printer produced all nineteen pages of her eight-hour business law final. She had twenty minutes to spare before it had to be turned in, and she was exhausted. The last page printed, and she stapled the document together. She pushed her chair out from her carrel in the library and headed toward the conference room where she had to turn the exam in. It wasn't a long walk, but after eight hours of sitting, it felt good to get up and move again.

She placed her exam under the punch clock to prove when she had turned it in and placed it in the drop box, then she pulled out her phone for the first time since the exam had started. She had a slightly belated good luck text from Jorge that she hadn't seen, but that wasn't what she was interested in. Instead, she flipped over to her texts with Gwen. They hadn't been able to get together for almost three weeks thanks to Etta's exams. She'd taken a week to study, and the exam window was ten days. Gwen had seemed a bit distant, but Etta had been too wrapped up in her exams to think about it.

She texted Gwen *hell week is over* before she stuck her phone in her pocket and headed back to the library to collect her things before heading home. She didn't think she'd have to wait long for an answer. Gwen never let her texts linger unless she was focusing on something at work.

Etta was halfway to the student parking lot before she realized she hadn't gotten a text back. She shifted her backpack to her other shoulder and pulled her phone out of her pocket. Her text had been delivered. Gwen simply hadn't gotten back to her yet. Maybe she was busy.

As she turned the corner, she saw someone leaning against the back of her car. She looked closer and saw that it was Gwen. Something fluttered in her chest, but she didn't have the energy to walk any faster.

Even though she was happy to see Gwen, she trudged up the hill to her car.

"You're here." Etta knew it was obvious, but her brain wasn't capable of much more than that.

"I am." Gwen stepped closer to Etta.

"Why?" Etta thought the question might be rude, but she couldn't tell anymore.

"There was a committee meeting tonight, so I was in the area. You said you were taking your last exam. I thought I might make you dinner." Gwen reached for Etta's backpack strap and slid it off her shoulder. With exams over, the backpack was mostly empty, but it was still a relief to not be wearing it.

Etta still couldn't believe that Gwen was standing in front of her. "Dinner?"

"Yes," Gwen laughed a little. "Dinner. I'm saving you from the overprocessed Chinese you were probably planning on ordering."

"Pizza. And I don't have any food at my apartment." Etta's brain was slowly starting to work again.

"I went to the grocery store. Now, get in your car so I can

follow you back to your place." Gwen leaned in and placed a light kiss on Etta's lips before pulling away.

"Okay." Etta blinked a few times before shaking her head. The movement brought her back to herself a little, and then she noticed that Gwen was parked next to her in the mostly empty parking lot. She really hoped Gwen didn't expect sex that night. She didn't think she was coordinated enough to make the effort. With another blink, she pulled her car keys out of her pocket and unlocked her car. Gwen opened her back seat and placed her backpack into it. Then she closed the door.

"I'll see you in a few minutes. Don't drive into anything on your way, all right?" Gwen said.

"Okay." Etta nodded and closed her car door. She was so glad that she lived near campus. She didn't know if she could survive a drive of more than ten minutes at that moment. She turned her car on, put it into reverse, and backed out of the parking spot. As she pointed her car toward the main road, she saw Gwen in her rearview mirror. Ten minutes. She only had to make it ten minutes and then she could collapse.

❖

Gwen didn't know what had possessed her to surprise Etta after her last exam of the semester. She was supposed to be pulling back, not finding excuses to spend time with Etta. Her plan to cut back on her texting with Etta had spectacularly backfired. She had missed Etta while she was distracted by finals, and she had taken the first opportunity to see her again. This was getting dangerous.

Still, it seemed like a waste to drive all the way to Cartersville and not see her. Her brain said she could have waited until Etta moved to Atlanta for the summer. That it was only a week away. But she had found herself at the grocery store anyway. She didn't buy anything fancy or impressive, but there were vegetables involved, and fewer preservatives. Her plan essentially amounted to salad and spaghetti and meatballs. She had a feeling that Etta wouldn't care if the pasta sauce came from a jar, but Gwen would make the meatballs herself.

She watched Etta pull into her driveway, so Gwen pulled into a space on the street. She quickly grabbed the grocery bags, locked her car, and caught up with Etta at the door that led to the stairs outside of her apartment.

Etta still looked exhausted and a little brain dead. Gwen didn't care. It was simply good to see her again.

Etta let them both into the apartment without saying anything. She dropped her backpack by the door, then walked over to the couch and collapsed. She closed her eyes for a minute, and while Gwen was waiting on her to open them again, she put the grocery bags down on the counter.

"There are pots and pans in the lower cabinet next to the sink," Etta said with her eyes still closed. She waved an arm in the general direction of the kitchen. Then she slowly opened her eyes. "You're really here, aren't you?"

"I am." Gwen walked over to the couch and reached out to brush some of Etta's hair off her forehead. "You should take a nap. I'll wake you up when the food is ready."

"Really?" Etta asked.

"Really. Go to sleep." Gwen remembered her own law school exams and how exhausting they were. 2L year was the worst. She was happy to make sure Etta was feeling a little more human before she had to leave for the night.

Etta hummed and closed her eyes again. She toed her shoes off and tucked her legs up onto the couch with her. Gwen returned to the kitchen to start pulling out everything necessary for her to start cooking. By the time she had found everything and set it out on the counter, Etta was asleep.

❖

Etta woke up to an amazing smell suffusing her apartment. As she opened her eyes, she saw Gwen sitting at her counter and scrolling through her phone. She shifted into a sitting position, and

Gwen turned at the noise. She smiled when she saw that Etta was awake.

"How long was I out?" Etta was still a little dazed, but her stomach was starting to make its presence known. She rubbed a hand over her face.

"About forty-five minutes," Gwen answered. "I was going to wake you soon. The meatballs are keeping warm in that pot, and the pasta can be ready in ten minutes. You looked like you needed to sleep more than you needed to eat."

"I think my stomach disagrees with that assessment." Etta pushed herself off the couch and toward Gwen. A few steps took her to Gwen's side. She put her hands on Gwen's hips and leaned in for a kiss, which Gwen granted. "Are you planning on staying?"

"I can't. I have a client meeting first thing in the morning, but I wanted to make sure you would survive the night." Gwen smiled at Etta.

"You didn't have to do that. I would have been okay with delivery pizza. I mean, this smells better, but I would have made it." Etta took half a step forward and pressed herself against Gwen. Gwen draped her arms around Etta's neck and kissed her much more thoroughly than before.

After a minute, Etta groaned and pulled away. "That's really, really nice, but if I don't eat something soon, I'm going to pass out."

"Sit down at the counter and I'll cook the pasta." Gwen pushed Etta toward one of the barstools. She stood up. As Etta left the kitchen, Gwen reentered it, then turned to the pot of warm water and increased the heat. It quickly started boiling, and once it did, she put the spaghetti in.

Etta watched her cook with interest. "You're good at that."

"It's pasta," Gwen said with a smile.

"No, I mean, that night you cooked that chicken, and now, with the meatballs." Etta used her hand to gesture at the meal. "I wouldn't know where to start with either of them."

"It's practice. And interest," Gwen said. "We had a cook while I was growing up, and I was fascinated. She taught me the basics. And my parents were happy that I wasn't getting into trouble like

Judith. She's my eldest sister and she liked to push all of my parents' buttons when she was a teenager. If I was making coq au vin, then I wasn't threatening to drop out of college, never mind that Judith was seven years older than me."

"She sounds fun." Etta smiled.

"She's mellowed a bit as she's gotten older, but she still thinks that the world should order itself around what she wants. Luckily, she normally wants positive things." Gwen wasn't sure how Judith would feel about Etta, but she didn't plan on having them meet any time soon. That way lay madness. "Do you have any siblings?"

"Nope. Just me." Etta shifted on the barstool. "My parents decided one was enough." She looked at the cooking pasta, trying to gauge if it was done entirely by sight. "You've got sisters?"

"Two. The aforementioned Judith, the hellion, and Lillian, who was absolutely my parents' favorite until she got pregnant without getting married first. They were angry about that for a while. Then I gave them something to be even angrier about, and by all accounts, they've come around." Gwen stirred the pasta, breaking eye contact with Etta.

"You don't know if they've come around?" Etta sensed that she needed to tread lightly, but she was too curious to let the subject drop entirely.

"I haven't spoken to my parents since I was nineteen." Gwen gave the pasta another stir seemingly fascinated by the boiling water.

"Nineteen?" Etta couldn't stop herself from saying it even though she probably shouldn't have.

Gwen picked up the pot of pasta water and poured it into a colander. She asked, "Do you have tongs?" without looking at Etta. It made Etta blink.

"Yeah. They're in the drawer in front of you." She was experiencing whiplash from the extreme change in subject.

Gwen pulled the tongs out and then opened the cabinets until she found two large bowls. She took them down, then turned back to Etta. She worked the muscle in her jaw. "I started dating a girl my sophomore year of college. They found out and disowned me."

"Jesus," Etta breathed out.

"They tried to get me kicked out of school. My mother said she wouldn't speak to me again until I came to my senses. She tried once I married David, but I refused her overtures. Being married didn't make me any less bisexual, so why would I let her back into my life?" Gwen took a deep breath then let it out slowly. "Judith already had access to the trust fund our grandparents set up for us, so she made sure I stayed in college. And she paid for law school."

"That's…" Etta looked at Gwen with sympathy. She didn't know what to say.

"We should eat before everything gets cold." Gwen gestured toward the food.

"My dad died when I was sixteen." The words spilled out of Etta's mouth.

"What?" Gwen stopped short and looked at Etta in confusion.

"Well, you've told me about your divorce, and your parents, and those are pretty personal things, and I realized I hadn't told you much about me in return, so…" Etta didn't know how to finish her thought.

"That's—" Gwen paused. "Thank you for telling me." She looked at Etta intently. "I'm sorry I haven't asked."

"No worries. And you're right. We should probably eat before everything gets cold." It was the only way Etta knew to redirect the conversation away from all of the depressing things they were talking about. She got up from where she was sitting and walked around the counter until she was standing next to Gwen. With a small smile, she took Gwen's hand and lifted it to her lips, placing a light kiss against her knuckles.

Without further conversation, they put the pasta into bowls with sauce and meatballs, then carried them around to the other side of the counter where they could sit and eat. Etta hooked her ankle around Gwen's and got a smile in return.

Chapter Eight

J orge, it's all of an hour and a half and the place is already furnished. I'm taking two suitcases and a box of books. Your presence here is unnecessary." Etta looked up at Jorge with a smile on her face. He really was very sweet, but she didn't need his help moving. "I can carry those things myself and you'll just have to turn around and drive back."

"Nope. You're not going to stop me," Jorge said. It seemed like he was determined to help her even if she didn't need it. "I'm following you up there and I'll carry your box of books inside for you."

"Fine." She punched him on the shoulder. "But you can carry the suitcases. They're heavier than the box of books."

"Whatever you want." He rolled one of Etta's suitcases to her car. He grunted when he went to pick it up. "What do you have in here? More books?"

"Just clothes," Etta replied as she looked at him in exasperation. "You can handle it. You asked for this, after all."

"Okay, okay." He heaved the first suitcase and then the second into the trunk of her car before he closed it. Then he grabbed the box of books and placed it in the back seat. "There you go. I have the address. I'll see you up there?"

"You'll see me up there. I'm going to stop and grab a six-pack once we get to town, and then we can find the best pizza place in all of East Atlanta Village. It's the least I can do since you're helping me move." She placed scare quotes with her fingers around the word helping.

"Damn right you will. My muscles are going to require protein after I lift those suitcases back out of your trunk." He clapped her on the back. She pushed him away from her.

"Get in your car and drive. I'll see you in ninety minutes." Despite not needing his help, Etta was glad he was coming. He and Dom were going to Savannah for the summer, so they probably wouldn't see each other again until school started at the end of August. He was going to be working in the Chatham County District Attorney's office and Dom was going to be working with the public defender. Etta couldn't wait to hear their stories about going up against each other in court. It was bound to be hilarious.

Etta slid behind the driver's seat in her car. Ninety minutes and she would be in Atlanta for the summer. Despite her trepidation about working at Dunleavy Byrd, she was excited by the move. It was a new neighborhood to explore, and she'd probably get to see Grey at least a few times over the summer. Plus, there was Gwen. She didn't know where that was going, but she was determined to enjoy the ride as long as it went on.

❖

Etta lounged on the couch in the one-bedroom house she was renting in East Atlanta Village. The rent was ridiculous, but not quite as ridiculous as what she would have been paying to live in a studio in one of the high-rises in Midtown that the firm had recommended. Sure, she might have been able to walk to work, but it wasn't worth the tradeoffs. In EAV, she felt like she was in an actual neighborhood.

Jorge had left a couple of hours earlier. He had already texted her that he was back in Cartersville, so she wasn't worried about him hitting a deer or something on his way back anymore. She had turned on the TV, but she didn't watch much TV in general, and nothing had caught her eye even though she was pretty sure that the house came with a cable package that included every channel ever.

She picked up her phone and switched to her string of texts with Gwen.

She sent *I'm officially all moved in* and waited for a response. She only had to wait a few minutes.

Is that an invitation to see your new place? Gwen texted back.

Etta hadn't been exactly sure what her aim had been when she sent the text, but now that Gwen had responded she realized that was exactly what she wanted.

It absolutely is. Etta added her address and tapped on the send icon.

She got *give me half an hour* back. She acknowledged the text, then tossed her phone down on the couch next to her. She looked around the apartment to see if anything needed to be cleaned up, but in the few hours she had been there, she hadn't made a mess. Her suitcases were unpacked though her books were still in their box. Taking them out would keep her busy for a few minutes at least. She got up from the couch and went over to the open box, flipping the top open. Now, she just had to find a place to put all of them.

❖

Finding parking in EAV on a Saturday night was nearly impossible and Gwen drove in circles for far longer than she liked before she found somewhere close to Etta's small house. But she did find something eventually. It was a short walk and soon she was walking up the stairs and onto the porch. She knocked on the door and shifted the bottle of wine she was holding from one hand to the other.

Etta opened the door with a smile on her face.

"Hey." Etta stepped back so Gwen could enter the house.

"Hello." Gwen leaned in and kissed Etta as the door closed behind her. Etta wrapped her arms around Gwen's neck and prolonged the kiss.

"I feel like I haven't seen you in forever," Etta said as she nuzzled against Gwen's cheek.

"It's been a week and a half." Gwen chuckled. She slowly

stepped away from Etta. "I know the cliché is a plant for a housewarming gift, but since you're only going to be here for a couple of months, and I don't know where to buy a plant at nine p.m. on a Saturday, I brought wine." She held the bottle out.

"The wine is definitely appreciated. The only other thing I have to drink here is three beers from earlier and tap water." Etta took the still cold bottle of white wine from Gwen's hand. "Now, we just have to find the glasses."

Etta laced their fingers together and tugged Gwen into the kitchen behind her.

"I suppose it was too much to hope that the cabinets would have glass fronts," Gwen said as she started opening the kitchen cabinets. As it was a small kitchen, it didn't take the two of them long to complete the search.

"I didn't find wine glasses, but I did find these," Etta said as she pulled out two short tumblers. "Hopefully, there's a corkscrew around here somewhere."

"Not necessary. It's a screw top." Gwen nodded toward the bottle in Etta's hand.

"Are you even allowed to like screw top wines?" Etta teased.

"I'm hardly going to cellar a sauvignon blanc, so it isn't going to matter. It's a good wine for a late spring evening, but I didn't spend a fortune on it." Gwen took the bottle from Etta's hand and opened it with a twist of her wrist. It only took a moment for her to pour the wine into the two tumblers.

"Do you have a wine cellar hidden in your condo somewhere?" Etta hadn't really explored Gwen's condo the one time she had been there, so it was entirely possible if not plausible.

"No, but when Christian was growing up, I lived in a too big house in Tuxedo Park and part of the basement was full of wine. David got it all in the divorce and I was happy to give it up. He was always more invested in it than I was. He collected bottles for their resale value. I simply like to drink it."

"David sounds like a prick," Etta said. Gwen laughed as she handed Etta one of the tumblers.

"We were happy for a while." Gwen sipped her wine. "But

looking back on it, that's a very good way to describe him. I always have had better taste in women than men."

"I hope I'm included in that." Etta stepped closer to Gwen and put her tumbler on the counter before pressing Gwen against it. Gwen's breath hitched.

"You certainly are." Gwen put her own glass down and wrapped her arms around Etta as Etta started kissing her way up Gwen's neck. She tugged Gwen's earlobe into her mouth and bit down lightly before letting it go.

"Maybe we should find the bed and you can show me what a good idea I am," Etta murmured.

"This house can't be more than seven hundred square feet. I have confidence in our ability to navigate it." Gwen kissed Etta again and pushed them both away from the counter.

It turned out Gwen was right and finding the bedroom was easier than figuring out where the glasses had been. They fell into bed a minute later.

CHAPTER NINE

How was your first day? Gwen's text came into Etta's phone just as she was getting in for the night. She tossed her keys onto the table by the door and put her backpack down underneath it. The firm didn't encourage taking work home, so she wouldn't need it. If she had to pull late nights, she'd have to do it at the office.

Her first day had been all tours. There was a tour of the building. There was a tour of the firm's offices. There was a tour of the department she was going to be working in for her first rotation. Her brain was swimming with it all. She'd barely managed to find the elevator to take her to the parking garage under the tower and back to her car.

She pressed the button to call Gwen. Right now, she needed to hear a friendly voice. "The entire place is overwhelming," she said as soon as the call connected. "The building is too big and I'm never going to be able to remember everyone's names. I'm going to be reviewing contracts for two weeks before they let me do anything more interesting, and the guy in charge of the section seems sleazy. I mean, I've only known him for half a day, but yeah, he has a sleazeball vibe." Etta toed off her shoes and threw herself down on the couch.

"That sounds terrible. I don't know if things will get better, but at the very least you'll learn your way around the building." Gwen was clearly going for something soothing, but it didn't make Etta feel that much better.

"Yeah, I know where my cubicle is and how to get to the

cafeteria, and that's it." Etta felt incredibly frustrated. She hoped things would get better, but she didn't think they would. At least, they wouldn't for the first two weeks. Maybe when they gave her something more interesting to do, things would improve.

"I hate to break it to you, but knowing where the cafeteria is probably won't matter. Every firm I know takes their summer associates out for lunch almost every day. And dinner sometimes too. Drinks." It sounded like Gwen was trying not to laugh.

"Where do you take your summer associates to lunch? I want to be prepared for the experience before it happens," Etta grumbled.

"The appeals section where I work doesn't have summer associates," Gwen replied.

"Really?" That made Etta curious. She thought that having an extra set of hands to do the scut work would be something people wanted.

"I'll occasionally poach one of the first-year associates from the general litigation section if they show promise, particularly if they've done a clerkship, but by the time a summer associate gets up to speed on our cases and understands our arguments, their rotation is generally over. If I do have something a law student could do, I send it down through the general litigation section and someone there supervises," Gwen said.

"Tell me you don't like baby lawyers without telling me you don't like baby lawyers." Etta laughed. She wasn't insulted; she wouldn't have trusted most of her classmates with important appellate litigation either.

"It isn't that I don't like young lawyers."

"You just don't have any use for them." Etta completed Gwen's thought.

"Not particularly. I do host a dinner party for the summer associates at the end of every summer. A few of the attorneys from the appeals section come and the managing director of the firm shows up, though normally he leaves after drinks. It's my contribution to the networking part of the process, which is as important as the actual work you'll do," Gwen said.

"I hate networking." Etta shuddered.

"Well, you've signed up for a summer of it," Gwen replied.

"I know. I know. Can we talk about something else? This is depressing me," Etta said.

"We can talk about anything you like." Gwen's good humor shone through in her voice.

"Thank you." Etta closed her eyes and allowed herself to relax a little more. She needed to decompress from her day, and talking to Gwen was an excellent way to do it.

❖

"Hey, Monroe!" Everett Harper, Etta's supervisor, called from his office. Why he couldn't seem to remember her first name, she wasn't sure, though truthfully, she wished he would forget her name entirely. She stood up, grabbed a legal pad, and stepped into his office.

"Yes, sir?" She put on her best fake smile. It was Wednesday and she already knew she didn't want to go into mergers and acquisitions. This guy was the reason why.

"I need you to run these contracts up to appeals. They need the signed originals, and for some reason they got routed here instead of up there." He thrust a manila folder in Etta's direction.

"Who should I give them to?" Etta didn't know the firm well enough yet to make that call.

"Whoever you see first. Just don't let the dragon lady catch you up there with them. In fact, don't let her catch you on the floor at all. She can be a real you-know-what sometimes, you know?" Everett shook the papers again and Etta grabbed them before they could spill out of the folder.

"Yes, sir." Etta turned and left his office. When a man she had just met told her that a woman she'd never met was a bitch, she took it with a large grain of salt. In her experience, she'd rarely found the assessment to line up with her own impressions.

As she was walking through the open area between offices, one of the first-year associates waved her over. Etta stopped by her desk while she wondered what she might want.

"Everett's decided you're his sacrificial lamb today?" Monica nodded at the folder in Etta's hand.

"I guess?" Etta replied.

"He needed to take those contacts up there last week and he forgot. He's hoping that if anyone gets yelled at, it'll be you and not him." Monica looked at her sympathetically.

"Is the head of appeals really that bad?" Etta asked. She trusted Monica's opinion slightly more than Everett's. It was less likely to be steeped in sexism.

Monica shrugged. "I've never had a reason to go up there. I saw her at the holiday party, but I didn't talk to her. I don't have any interest in litigation. Some people like her. A lot of people don't. A lot of those people are like Everett, though, so who knows? She has a reputation as a hard ass, but the appeals section is probably the most successful part of the firm, so…" Monica looked up as if she could see through the ceiling all the way to the floor that held the appeals section. "There are rumors that she's trying to get appointed to the state supreme court, so she might not be here much longer to yell at anyone. I'd avoid her entirely if I were you. Just give the papers to the first administrative assistant that you see and get out of there."

"Uh, thanks." Now Etta didn't know what to believe. But she knew she didn't want to get yelled at for something that wasn't her fault. She hadn't even been at the firm when Everett had forgotten about the contracts.

She headed toward the elevators and pressed the up button. A door opened almost immediately, and the three-floor ride took no time at all. She stepped out of the elevator and into the vestibule. A quick look around had her making a right turn toward where she heard voices. She stepped up to the first cubicle that she saw.

"Excuse me?" she asked. Etta didn't want to interrupt someone who had nothing to do with the papers in her hand, but she also didn't know who might be working on that case. Everett had been singularly unhelpful.

"Yes?" An older woman looked up from her computer. "May I help you?"

"Mr. Harper told me to give these papers to someone in this section, but he didn't tell me who needed them." Etta held the papers out.

The woman flipped the folder open and scanned the pages. "You'll need to take these to Ms. Strickland directly." She closed the folder and handed it back to Etta.

"And Ms. Strickland is...?" Etta looked around to see if there was a nameplate anywhere that might give her a clue about where Ms. Strickland might be located.

"The corner office, hon. She's the section head." The woman didn't say it like Etta should be afraid for her life, so that was promising. Still, Etta's stomach churned. She didn't normally get so nervous about meeting new people, but she didn't know what she was walking into either. Would Ms. Strickland shoot the messenger, or would she realize that it wasn't Etta's mistake?

"She's not that fearsome," the woman said, clearly sensing Etta's reaction. "Just go up to her administrative assistant and tell them you have the Martinez contracts for her. Sam will let you know if you can leave them or if she needs to talk to you about something."

"Right." Etta flashed a smile. "Thank you."

"You're welcome." The woman turned to her computer and went back to work. Etta took that as a dismissal and headed toward the impressive-looking office at the corner of the building.

Etta stopped in front of the doors that insulated the corner office from the rest of the floor. With a deep breath, she opened them and stepped inside. It was cooler in the office, and something about it smelled familiar. Etta took a deep breath and tried to place the scent.

"Can I help you?" Sam looked a lot younger than Etta had anticipated, and their hair was puffed up in an afro that did not say corporate law. Neither did their red plaid pants and the corset they were wearing over their button-down shirt. Etta blinked, readjusted her assumptions about the dragon lady in the corner office, and approached the desk.

"I have the Martinez contracts, and I was told I should give them to you." Etta held the folder out.

"Ms. Strickland will want to talk to you about those. You can have a seat. It might be a minute." Sam pointed toward a chair that Etta anxiously sank into. Then they picked up the phone. After a brief conversation, Sam looked at Etta again. "She said it would be at least five minutes, but that you should wait."

Etta nodded from her seat. If one of the firm's senior partners wanted her to wait for her, she would do that. Anything else would probably be career suicide. She pulled out her phone and sent a text to Gwen.

Apparently, I'm about to meet the scariest person at the firm. Any advice?

Etta didn't expect a real answer during the workday, but it gave her something to do with her hands and bled off some of her nervous energy. Etta tried not to fidget as she waited. It would be fine. She would drop off the contracts, and even if the infamous Ms. Strickland decided to lay into her, she would be fine. What was the saying about words never hurting? She knew she hadn't done anything wrong.

After another few minutes of sitting, the light on Sam's phone flashed. They picked it up and had another brief conversation before turning to Etta.

"You can go in now." Sam motioned toward the door with their head.

"Thanks." Etta tried to smile at them as she walked past their desk and opened the imposing door in front of her.

The first thing Etta saw as she stepped into the office was the view. Midtown Atlanta sprawled out in front of her. Then she remembered she was in the office to meet with someone. She turned toward the desk. When she saw who was sitting at it, she nearly had a heart attack.

❖

Gwen was staring at her computer at an email that had just come in when she felt the change in the atmosphere that signaled her office door had opened. "So, who has Everett sent up here to take the fall for his incompetence?" she said, still scanning the email.

When she didn't hear an immediate reply, she finally looked away from her computer.

It only took a second for her to recognize Etta standing in front of her, but after that, her brain came to a complete, stuttering stop. It left her staring at Etta, unable to say anything.

It seemed like Etta was suffering from the same condition, though, as she wasn't saying anything either. They stared at each other for a long minute. Gwen's cell phone vibrated on her desktop and it jarred Gwen back to reality. She looked down at it and then back at Etta.

"You have my contracts?" Gwen didn't know what else to say. This was bad. This was so very bad. There was a strong taboo at the firm against having sex with subordinates. One that she fully supported. One that she had thoroughly broken. She held her hand out for the contracts. She didn't know what else to do. Her brain hadn't caught up yet.

Somehow, that was enough to spur Etta into action. She held the folder out in response. "I do." She looked like she still hadn't processed that Gwen was sitting on the other side of the desk.

"Thank you." Gwen took the folder and opened it just long enough to make sure it contained the documents she wanted. She placed the folder down on her desk. "Clearly, we need to have a discussion." They couldn't keep doing what they were doing and act like this new information didn't matter. Things had changed, but Gwen wasn't processing things quickly enough to figure out what it meant.

"Yeah." Etta swallowed. She was starting to look dazed.

"If it's all right with you, I'll come over tonight. We shouldn't talk about this here." Gwen tried to pull herself together. One of them had to take charge of the situation, and it looked like it was going to be her.

"Yeah. Yeah, that works." Etta shook her head as if trying to clear it. "I should—" Etta rubbed her forehead. "I'm going to go now. Back downstairs. I have contracts to review." Etta didn't wait for Gwen to dismiss her. She turned and walked out of the door without looking back.

Chapter Ten

G rey, I need you to call me back the second you get this message. I'm not kidding." Gwen ended the call on her phone and texted the same thing. Half an hour had passed since Etta had left her office and Gwen had finally come back to herself. Except now that she could think clearly again, she didn't know what to think. She didn't know what to do. She had no idea what she was going to say to Etta that night.

Her phone rang.

It was Grey.

Gwen sighed in relief and answered the call. Maybe Grey would know what to do.

"Grey, I'm having a legitimate crisis," Gwen said as the call connected.

"Whoa. Okay. What's going on?" Grey sounded calm, which only made Gwen more agitated.

"The law student. *My* law student." Gwen ran her hand through her hair.

"Don't tell me you've fallen in love with her or something, because I warned you about that," Grey said.

"It's significantly worse than that. She's here." Gwen felt like she was unraveling.

"Like, in your office? Has she turned into some sort of stalker?" Now, Grey sounded worried.

"No, no. Not like that. She's a summer associate at the firm. She's down in M&A right now reviewing contracts. Or at least pretending to review contracts, because she somehow looked even more shocked about this than I am."

"Wait, she's working there?" Grey asked.

"Yes. She's basically an intern. I'm fucking one of the interns. Do you know how bad that looks?" Gwen felt hysterical. She felt like the world was unraveling.

"Yeah, that does not look good. And *I didn't know* is a pretty flimsy excuse," Grey said.

"Yes, I'm aware." Gwen started pacing.

"Well, you can't do it again, obviously."

Grey made it sound so simple. Maybe it was that simple. She'd go to Etta's house that night and tell her that whatever they had been doing was over. That things had to end to protect both of them. Gwen didn't want to be seen as taking advantage of Etta. Etta didn't want to seem to be getting favors in return for sex. Everything had to end.

"You're right. Of course, you're right." Gwen took a deep breath, exhaled, and then took another one.

"I know I am. It's going to be fine. You'll talk to her and then you won't see her again for the rest of the summer. It isn't like you even have summer associates. You can avoid each other for the next two months. It'll be okay," Grey said.

"Thank you." Gwen stopped pacing. "Thank you for helping me not completely spiral about this."

"It's no problem. Now, I have to deal with work stuff. The caterer for the annual gala needs to have a discussion about the appetizers," Grey said.

"Good luck," Gwen replied.

"You too." Grey hung up and left Gwen standing in the middle of her office. She didn't want to go back to work. She still felt too scattered for that. Oral arguments wouldn't wait on her to figure out her life, though. She needed to finish writing what she would say. They were practicing arguments on Friday morning. She needed to know everything about the case inside and out before then.

❖

Etta sat at her computer staring at the screen. She didn't know what she was supposed to do now. Ostensibly, she was reviewing a confidentiality agreement to make sure it was thorough enough to protect their client's interests in a merger. In reality, she wasn't doing anything.

Gwen was a partner. She was a senior partner at Dunleavy Byrd. She wasn't Etta's boss, but she could definitely make things about this summer harder for Etta. Etta didn't think that she would, but even the idea that she could gave Etta pause.

"Hey, Etta, are you okay?" Monica asked as she stopped by Etta's cubicle. "You look a little dazed. Did they give you a hard time up in appeals?"

"Uh, no. No, everyone up there was helpful. Nice, even. I, uh, met the section head. She sounded like she wanted to give Everett a hard time, but she didn't yell at me or anything." Somehow it was worse. Gwen had barely reacted to finding Etta in her office. She had asked for the contracts while Etta was melting down. Etta didn't know how Gwen could be so calm about everything. She guessed she'd get a chance to ask after work that day.

"Good. I'm glad it worked out." Monica smiled at Etta. "Some of the first-year associates go out for drinks Thursdays after work. You should come tomorrow."

"Yeah, I'll think about it. Let me know where you're going." Etta answered automatically. She didn't feel capable of making decisions about socializing or networking at the moment. She had a bigger problem to navigate. "Do you know what time the senior partners leave at the end of the day?"

Etta's day ended at five, but she assumed the senior partners could make their own hours.

"Depends on who it is. Erika takes off around four, but she also gets here at six, so she probably isn't the best example." Erika was the M&A section chief. Etta had met her briefly when she had first been introduced to the department, but she hadn't seen her since then. "And I don't know about anyone else. Don't worry about staying late to impress people. That's for your first year as an associate, not this summer."

"Right, thanks." Etta didn't know how to ask more specifically about Gwen without Monica wanting to know why she was asking, and she probably didn't know anything anyway.

"You'll be fine. Enjoy the summer." Monica pushed away from the cubicle wall and headed back to her own workstation.

Etta went back to freaking out.

❖

Etta pulled into the parking space next to her house and saw a figure sitting on her front porch steps. A closer look showed her it was Gwen, still in her clothes from the office. Etta got out of her car and slowly approached the front door. She didn't know what Gwen was going to say, but she had a feeling she wasn't going to like it. All she felt was dread.

Gwen stood once Etta got a few feet away. She had a pizza box in her hands.

"I thought about bringing bourbon, but that seemed like a bad idea." Gwen nodded down at the pizza box.

"How long have you been out here?" Etta asked. It seemed weird that Gwen would be waiting for her at all. She had expected her to show up much later, and definitely not with food.

"Only about five minutes. I tried to time it where I wouldn't get here until after you'd gotten home, but the pizza got finished faster than I anticipated." Gwen looked worried, but Etta wasn't quite sure what she was worried about.

Etta slid past Gwen and pulled out her keys to unlock the door. Gwen followed her inside without being invited. She carried the pizza into the kitchen, put it down on the counter, and then turned toward Etta.

"This is where you tell me we can't do this anymore, isn't it?" Etta asked. Gwen couldn't intend to do anything other than break off their relationship. Not that they really had a relationship. They had sex. Occasionally they talked. They'd never been on a date. They'd never really done anything together at all. Ending that shouldn't hurt, but somehow it did.

"Yeah, that's what I was going to say. It looks terrible. If anyone found out, it would be bad for both of us." Gwen looked as resigned as Etta felt.

"You're not going to get me fired, are you?" Etta didn't think Gwen would, but she felt compelled to ask anyway.

"Absolutely not." Gwen looked horrified at the idea. "You can finish your summer rotations as usual, assuming you want to. I don't have anything to do with the summer associates."

"Yeah. I mean, I'm not having the greatest time, but I said I'd do it. I don't have any plans to quit. I'm just hoping things get more interesting after I rotate out of M&A." Etta shrugged helplessly.

Gwen rubbed her forehead. "Everett's an asshole. Unfortunately, he came in when the firm acquired another firm, and we can't fire him for another two years without paying him more than he's worth." She sighed and rubbed her forehead. "And I didn't tell you any of that."

"When the 3Ls told me to find someone who knew where the bodies were buried, I don't think they had this in mind," Etta said.

"No, probably not," Gwen replied.

"I wish I had some of that bourbon you didn't bring." Etta closed her eyes. "This is a mess."

"Yes. It is."

"Is it true you're trying to get appointed to the state supreme court?" Etta didn't know why that suddenly occurred to her, but she couldn't think of anything else to say.

"Yes, though I didn't know that rumor was out there already." Gwen pursed her lips. Etta wondered if that factored into her decision to break things off. As if they needed another reason.

"It is. I don't know how many people know, but yeah. I heard it from one of the first year associates. This would look really bad if the nominating commission found out about it, wouldn't it?" Etta asked.

"I would imagine so." Gwen looked like she was holding back on a desire to pace. Her muscles were tense. There wasn't room in the kitchen for pacing, though.

"Then it's good that there won't be anything for them to find out about," Etta said. There was no use in fighting for something that was already doomed.

Gwen looked out the kitchen window, though Etta had a feeling she wasn't really seeing what was on the other side. "Did I end up being the scariest person at the firm?" she asked.

"You're scary for so many reasons that have nothing at all to do with your reputation at the firm. But they did hype you up a lot. I didn't know you wore glasses." Etta reached out and caught part of Gwen's shirt between her fingers, brushing against her stomach as she did it. It caused Gwen to refocus on her. Etta couldn't stop herself from smiling.

"I'm a lawyer over forty. Reading glasses come with the territory." Gwen shifted until Etta was pressed against the counter. Etta took a shuddering breath and flattened her palm against Gwen's stomach before sliding it around to her back. She pulled Gwen in tighter against her.

"You know, we can't possibly fuck this up any more than it's already been fucked." Etta leaned in and captured Gwen's lips between her own.

Gwen breathed out and tried to step even closer. Despite the situation, the chemistry between them hadn't abated. Gwen opened her mouth to allow Etta's tongue inside. They kept trying to get closer as the heat built between them.

Finally, Etta pushed Gwen a few inches away. "My bedroom is five steps from here."

"That's a bad idea," Gwen whispered.

"This was always a bad idea," Etta replied. She kissed Gwen again. "Let's go to bed. We can stop having bad ideas in the morning."

With a groan, Gwen gave in.

❖

Gwen looked over at where Etta was asleep next to her in the bed. She wanted to stay. She wanted to wake up with Etta and indulge in lazy kisses first thing in the morning and lounge around in bed with her.

She couldn't.

It was almost morning. She needed to leave, to go home. They both would have to go to work in too few hours and then they would have to pretend that they had never done this. They would have to pretend like they had never met.

It was for the best.

Gwen slid out of bed and started getting dressed. Etta took a deep breath and rolled toward Gwen.

"You're leaving, aren't you?" she asked, voice still thick with sleep.

"I am," Gwen replied. She finished buttoning her shirt, lifting her hair out of the collar. She leaned down and kissed Etta lightly. "Go back to sleep."

"I don't want to." Etta opened her eyes and looked at Gwen.

"Goodbye, Etta." Gwen stepped away from the bed.

"Goodbye."

Gwen turned and left. She let herself out of the house and walked to her car. She wanted to go back. She couldn't go back. She got in her car and drove away.

Chapter Eleven

Gwen walked into her office in the morning to an envelope sitting in the middle of her desk. She had left early enough the day before that the mail hadn't been processed yet. The envelope hadn't been opened, which was unusual as Sam normally went through her mail for her, making sure everything was scanned and processed.

She picked it up and looked at the envelope. It had a return address from the Judicial Nominating Commission, which was probably why Sam hadn't opened it.

Gwen pulled out a letter opener and sliced through the paper with a definitive movement, then she pulled out the letter inside. It was several sheets of paper long. She unfolded it and scanned the first page. It was a letter acknowledging her statement of interest in the supreme court position with an enclosed application. She had seen the application before on the commission's website, but it was a different thing to be holding it in her hand. It was forty questions long, and it was going to take a significant amount of time to complete.

Gwen set the application aside. She would start working on it soon, but she still had oral arguments to prep for, and those had to come first.

❖

"So, are you coming to happy hour?" Monica asked as she passed Etta's cubicle.

"What?" Etta was absorbed in the contract she was reviewing. Focusing on that had been better than going over her night with Gwen repeatedly in her head.

"Happy hour?" Monica said again.

"Oh. Uh, yeah. Sure." It was something to keep her attention off Gwen, so she'd take it.

"Great. We go to a place called the Collection down the street. It's set up like one of those weird museum-of-curiosity places that you find in random old houses in the UK. I know it sounds pretentious, but the drinks are worth it. I'll warn you, it's going to be full of a lot of lawyers," Monica said.

"Sounds interesting." Etta tried to smile.

"If you can be by the elevators in five, I'll walk over with you." Monica seemed way too happy and energetic, but Etta knew that was her own mood reacting to what was probably a normal amount of enthusiasm.

"I'll be there." Etta nodded.

❖

Etta and Monica stepped through the door to the Collection and Etta looked around curiously. The place had a surprisingly high ceiling that was packed to the rafters with every random thing imaginable, from old books to taxidermized animals to succulents. There was a bright blue plastic bison head hanging on the far wall. There was a graffitied mural painted on the side of a staircase that led to who-knew-where. The bar was dark wood with a long, distressed mirror behind it. Bottles of alcohol were lined up in front of it. The crowd hadn't arrived yet, so there were only a smattering of people throughout the space.

"There's more seating in the back." Monica pointed before heading in that direction. Etta followed along behind her. True to her word, the back of the bar opened to a seating area full of booths around the edges and high-top tables in the center.

Monica snagged one of the tables and slid one of the menus

to Etta as Etta sat next to her. "Everyone else will be here in a few minutes."

"Great." Etta took the menu and looked over it. She was still trying to muster up some enthusiasm for the outing.

"Everything okay?" Monica asked with obvious concern.

"Yeah. Everything's fine." Etta was trying. She really was. "I didn't sleep well last night, so I'm not running at one hundred percent right now." At least that was the truth. She hadn't really fallen back asleep after Gwen had left.

"Understood." Monia nodded. "Let me buy you a drink and see if that helps. If not, no one is going to care if you head out early."

"Okay. Sure." Etta smiled. She could do this. Alcohol would help. She looked down at the menu. "What's a Space Daiquiri?"

Monica's eye lit up. "Just order it. Trust me."

"Uh, yeah, sure. I'll have a Space Daiquiri." Etta didn't know what she was getting herself into, but it was better than moping. Moping had never really been her thing. She'd be fine. She might never see Gwen again, but she'd be fine.

❖

"You're here late."

Gwen recognized Brad both through his voice and because no one else would dare enter her office without her permission.

"We're mooting the Fletcher case tomorrow. I want to make sure I'm ready." Gwen was sitting at her desk reading through the printed notes she would take to the podium with her in the morning. She wanted to make sure they were as perfect as they could be. She'd know more about what she needed to change after they practiced, but that didn't mean she wouldn't be as prepared as she would be if she was appearing before the state supreme court. Those arguments were on Wednesday. Everything needed to be locked in by then.

Still, she couldn't ignore Brad. She looked away from her notes and up at him. "Is there something I can help you with?"

"Yes. Come to dinner with me," Brad said.

"Brad, I don't have time." Gwen spread her arms to encompass all of the papers on her desk.

"You have to eat. Come on." He made a gesture with his head. "I'm craving steamed mussels and I don't want to go alone."

"Fine." Gwen tossed the papers down onto her desk, making it even more cluttered. She smiled at him. She really did like Brad, but sometimes his timing was terrible. "Is there a reason you're not having this meal with your wife?"

"She didn't want to drive to Midtown, and I have to come back here afterward too. I have a video conference with the people at Hironaka Enterprises in Osaka at eight."

"Time zones will kill you every time." Gwen came around from her desk and grabbed her purse. "Where are we going?"

"I thought we'd go to that French seafood place that's down the street. Fleur de Eau or whatever it is," Brad said.

"Fleur de Eau makes no sense, but I know where you're talking about." Gwen preceded Brad out of her office and headed toward the elevators.

"See, this is why I asked you. You keep me straight, Gwen. I don't know what I'm going to do without you." Brad clapped her on the shoulder.

"Don't say that. You'll jinx it." Gwen pressed the button to call the elevator.

❖

Etta was drunk. It turned out Space Daiquiris involved dry ice, a space shuttle–shaped plastic cup, and three kinds of rum. She'd had two. After that, the bartender had told her she wasn't allowed to order any more, so she'd switched to regular daiquiris with normal amounts of rum in them. Still, even those were enough to have the room spinning.

She felt loose and relaxed and she wasn't obsessing over Gwen anymore. At least, she'd gotten down to only thinking about Gwen every fifteen minutes instead of constantly.

"Come on." Monica stepped a few feet away from the table

and motioned Etta over. Etta followed her on unsteady legs. "So, I think I've finally had enough to drink to ask you if you'd like to go to dinner with me sometime."

Etta's brain tripped and it took her a second to catch up to what Monica was saying. "Like, on a date?" She felt the need to clarify exactly what they were talking about. She didn't want to get this wrong and her brain wasn't operating at one hundred percent.

"Yeah, like a date." Monica laughed nervously.

"Oh. Wow. I, um—" Etta blinked. She hadn't expected Monica to ask her out. She really, really hadn't. And she really wasn't ready to go on any dates. Even drunk she knew that much. "I don't think that's the best..."

"Right. No, totally," Monica rushed to fill the silence. "I get it. Dating people at work can be tricky. And you're only going to be around for the summer. I shouldn't have asked."

"No. It's fine. I mean, the answer is still no, but I'm not upset that you asked. I just got out of a thing, and yeah, work things are hard, and—" Etta rambled through an explanation.

"Yeah. I'm—" Monica looked at Etta more closely. "Are you okay to get home?"

"Huh? Oh, yeah, I'm going to grab an Uber or something. Don't worry, I'm not dumb enough to drive after two of those drinks that I'm pretty sure should be illegal," Etta reassured Monica.

"Okay. Good. Do you want me to wait with you until it gets here?" Monica asked.

"Nah, I'm okay. You can take off. I'm not going to be far behind you." Etta pulled out her phone. A few taps later and she had a car on the way. "See, I'm all set." She showed Monica the screen.

Monica laughed. "Yeah. I'll see you at work tomorrow. Drink some water." Monica picked up her purse and with a wave walked out of the bar. A minute later, Etta grabbed her own stuff and went outside to wait for her ride to get there. Half an hour later, she was unlocking her front door and stumbling into her bedroom. Work wasn't going to be fun the next day.

❖

Gwen delicately wiped her mouth with her napkin as she finished the last of her sea bass. She had tried all night not to think about the fact that Etta had once bartended in the restaurant where they were having dinner, but it was hard. She could picture Etta behind the bar making drinks and flirting with the customers.

This would have been easier if Etta had been nothing but a bartender. She never would have shown up at Gwen's firm. They could have continued to sleep together for as long as they had wanted. Now, everything was screwed up.

"Gwen, is everything okay?" Brad asked as he finished up his mussels.

"Hmm?" Gwen pulled her mind away from Etta and back to the current moment.

"You're quieter than usual," he prodded.

"Oh, I'm just distracted by this case. You know how I can get right before arguments." It wasn't like she could tell Brad what was really going on.

"Are you sure?" Brad looked at her as if he was trying to read her mind.

"I'm sure. I think after we get back to the office I'll head home. I'll do better looking at everything with fresh eyes in the morning." Gwen drank the rest of her wine.

"If you're sure?" Brad asked.

"I'm sure. Thank you for dragging me to dinner, though. You were right. I needed to eat something." She probably would have ordered something eventually, but the company had been nice.

"Well, then I'm glad I stopped by your office." Brad motioned for the check, and after taking care of it, waited for Gwen to stand before joining her on his feet. "I'll walk you to your car. Then I'm off to my meeting. You're right. Time zones will kill you."

They left the restaurant and made the short walk back to the underground garage where the Dunleavy Byrd employees all parked. Gwen walked toward her car touching the handle to unlock it. With a wave, Brad headed toward the elevators that would take him into the building. Gwen got into her car and headed home.

Chapter Twelve

Gwen stepped into the moot courtroom and looked around to make sure she was the first person there. She liked to get in the room early where she could get a feel for the atmosphere. She might have practiced oral arguments in it a hundred times, but every time she stepped in it, it felt different. Today, it was a little warmer than usual.

She looked up at the bench and imagined the justices on the Georgia State Supreme Court sitting up there behind the dark wood panels. This case was important enough that they would be simulating a full hearing with nine justices and opposing counsel. She would make her argument and reserve time for rebuttal. Lindsay, one of the other more senior attorneys in her section, would play the part of the appellee. They had worked together to determine what they thought the opposing side would say, but she was sure Lindsay would have a curveball or two to throw her way.

The Georgia State Supreme Court was known for being a hot bench, and the younger attorneys tasked with playing the justices had been instructed to act as such. She had a feeling she'd spend more of her time answering questions than she would reciting the arguments from her brief.

Gwen stepped up to the podium and put her binder down on it. She opened the cover and flipped through the pages, going through in her mind the points she wanted to make. These arguments in the Fletcher case were about standing. The appellee, the McGuire Corporation, was arguing that the Fletchers didn't have the right to sue them because the Fletchers hadn't been the ones hurt by them. It was a technical argument and unlikely to generate any media attention, but it could change who was allowed to bring a case in Georgia courts. It was important even if it wasn't flashy.

The door opened at the back of the room, and she turned to see who had joined her. It was Lindsay, the attorney playing the appellee. Lindsay, with a binder of her own tucked under an arm, walked up to the podium and offered Gwen her hand.

"I'm going to beat you this time," Lindsay said as Gwen returned her handshake.

"You have the better argument," Gwen acknowledged.

"Are you worried about this one?" Lindsay dropped the posturing.

"I worry about all of them, but the odds on this one don't look good." If the justices stuck to current law, Gwen knew that they were going to lose, but she thought she had a compelling argument to expand the law to give her clients the right to sue the McGuire Corporation. The stakes couldn't be higher as far as the Fletchers were concerned. If they won, the corporation would probably rush to settle. If they lost, the case was completely over.

"Still haven't found a silver bullet?" They both knew that at this point in the case, it was unlikely they would find something they had overlooked at one of the earlier stages.

"No. This case has always been a long shot, and the clients know that." Gwen looked up at the bench. "But my best friend recently reminded me that I'm the best damned appeals lawyer in the state. If anyone can win this, it's me." Gwen thrived when everything was resting on her shoulders.

"Well, on Wednesday, I'll be rooting for you. Today, I'm going to kick your ass." Lindsay smiled ruthlessly.

Gwen barked out a laugh. "Good luck with that. Enjoy it while it lasts." Lindsay might have a more conventional argument, but Gwen didn't like losing, and as Grey had said, she was very, very good at her job.

She took a seat at the appellant's table and waited for the justices and everyone who would be watching to arrive.

❖

Etta was running late. She nearly skidded her car into a parking space, jumped out of it, and ran to the elevators. There wasn't much she could do to make the elevator run faster, so she pulled out her phone to check her firm email. The latest message was from the director of the summer associate program telling all of them to be in the moot courtroom by eight thirty. Etta checked her watch. It was eight twenty-seven, and she didn't even know where the moot courtroom was.

The elevator opened and she stepped inside for the short ride into the building. From there, she'd have to take a second elevator to get to the floors where the firm was located. She checked her watch again. She wasn't going to make it in time.

❖

Gwen stood up at the podium as the justices took their seats on the bench. She gave them a moment to get settled, then began.

"May it…"

❖

Etta cracked open the door to the moot courtroom as quietly as she could. When she had it open enough to slip through, she stepped into the back of the courtroom and then into one of the seats at the back.

"…please the court."

Etta tried to discreetly take a deep breath to calm herself down from her rush to the courtroom. She hadn't missed much. It took her another second to realize it was Gwen speaking from the podium.

The first thing that popped into her mind was that she had never seen Gwen in a suit before. That wasn't why all of the summer associates were there to watch, though. Etta forced herself to pay attention to the argument.

By Etta's unofficial count, Gwen managed to speak uninter-
rupted for a whopping ninety seconds before one of the justices
interrupted her with a question. Well, it was more an opinion veiled
as a question than an actual question. Gwen appeared to be prepared
for it, though. She parried it with ease and pulled the conversation
back to her point.

She managed an even shorter statement before she got another
question, this one more legitimate than the previous question had
been. Gwen answered that one just as easily.

Etta tried to follow the argument, but she was hardly an expert
in Georgia civil procedure. Still, even she could tell that Gwen knew
what she was talking about backward and forward.

There were more questions, and even though Etta couldn't see
her face, Gwen's body language said she felt comfortable each time
the justices tried to trip her up. Eighteen minutes passed much faster
than Etta thought they would, and then Gwen was stepping away
from the podium and allowing the other attorney to take her place.

Etta slid back from the edge of her seat as some of the tension
left the room. Gwen was good. Gwen was really good. She was a
combination of charisma and wicked intelligence. Etta wasn't sure
how anyone could argue against her and win. As Etta waited for the
other attorney to begin her arguments, she kept her focus on Gwen.
She had a feeling she wasn't the only one.

❖

Gwen stepped away from the podium and looked over at
Lindsay as she took her place. She took a quick look around the
gallery as she found her seat. As it wasn't a real courtroom, the
gallery was much smaller than it would be when she was actually in
front of the supreme court. The other two attorneys she was working
with on the case were sitting directly on the other side of the bar
taking notes. She had drawn a smattering of people from the general
litigation section. Then she caught sight of the cadre of summer
associates sitting in the middle of the room. She hadn't expected
them, but she supposed she should have. The firm didn't often go to

this much trouble for a case. It would be good for the young lawyers to have the experience.

Finally, she saw Etta sitting in the very back of the room, right next to the door.

Their eyes met. Gwen felt the same spark of attraction she felt every time she saw Etta. As much as she wanted to be able to turn it off now that she knew Etta was untouchable, she couldn't. She flushed. Thinking about Etta in these circumstances was both inappropriate and dangerous.

Gwen turned away from Etta and back to Lindsay and her argument. She needed to pay attention to the case and not to her libido. She was certain that Lindsay was going to say something unpredictable, and she needed to be ready to counter it.

❖

Etta sucked in a breath as Gwen broke the eye contact they had been sharing. She felt jittery, like she had just downed a double shot of espresso. She had no idea what the other lawyer was saying. She was too busy staring at the back of Gwen's head while Gwen took notes.

The justices weren't any easier on the other lawyer than they had been on Gwen, but the words passed Etta by until she heard a collective intake of breath from the front of the courtroom. She focused again.

Gwen was writing something down and the two lawyers behind her were furiously taking notes. Gwen looked much less stressed than they did.

Again, the twenty minutes of the appellee's argument went faster than Etta expected it would, and then Gwen was up at the podium again. She only had two minutes left to convince the justices that she was right and that the other side was wrong.

Gwen paused for a moment then began, "I'm glad that the appellee brings up *Parker v. Leeuwenburg,* because in his dissent, Justice Hunstein clearly states—" and from there, she was off. Somehow, in two minutes, Gwen completely dissected the appellee's arguments. Etta looked around the room and it seemed like the other summer associates were impressed as well.

Etta was more than impressed. She was turned on. She wanted to get Gwen alone, shove her against a wall, pull down her hair, and pop open all of the buttons on her shirt where she could get at her skin. She needed to touch Gwen. It was a compulsion.

As soon as the timer went off indicating that Gwen was out of time, it felt like a rush of tension left the room. Gwen closed her binder and stepped away from the podium. She cleared her throat. "We'll reconvene in the main conference room on the fifteenth floor at one thirty," she announced.

Etta already knew that the summer associates weren't invited to the meeting. She would be back to reviewing contracts as soon as lunch was over.

Gwen was still at the front of the room talking to the opposing lawyer, but Etta couldn't hear what they were saying. The group of summer associates were all finding their feet and shuffling out of the room.

Etta needed to talk to Gwen. She wondered if she could get past Sam and into Gwen's office. There was only one way to find out.

Chapter Thirteen

G wen strode into her outer office only to come up short when she saw Etta sitting in one of the chairs reserved for people waiting to see her. She looked at Sam and raised an eyebrow in question. Sam looked at her like they didn't know what was going on either.

"Ms. Monroe, is there something I can do for you?" Gwen asked. Etta was bouncing one of her legs up and down and she looked agitated.

"Yes. Actually, the case you just mooted. I think I might have some insight." The words tumbled out of Etta's mouth.

Gwen looked at her skeptically. She wasn't sure being alone in her office with Etta right now was the best idea. Her body was still coming down from the rush of a successful argument and she was full of pent-up energy. She was planning on going on a walk during the lunch break just to get some of that energy out. But she didn't know how to extricate herself from this situation without entirely dismissing Etta while Sam watched. Despite her reputation, she tried not to be a complete bitch at work. She couldn't blow Etta off. Besides, Etta might have a genuine insight into the case. She couldn't risk missing that either.

"Come in then." Gwen motioned toward the door with her head and then opened it. She watched as Etta stood and followed her in. As soon as the door closed, and before she could say anything, she felt a hand grasp her wrist and tug. She spun around, ready to question what Etta might want, but before she could, Etta's lips were on hers.

She instinctively sank into the kiss, wrapping her arms around Etta as Etta pulled her close. Then Etta was forcing her to walk backward. It was only a few steps before she hit the edge of her desk, coming to rest against it. She slid onto it and spread her legs until they fit around Etta's hips. All the while, Etta kept kissing her, bringing their lips together without finesse.

All of Gwen's pent-up energy finally had an outlet.

She gasped as Etta started kissing her neck then moaned when Etta flexed her hand against her hips.

Hearing the moan brought her back to herself.

"We're not supposed to be doing this." She pushed Etta away, though not very far.

"Yeah, that's stupid." Etta kissed her more gently this time. Gwen kissed her back.

"This is a bad idea." Gwen tried again, but her heart wasn't in it. She arched forward against Etta as Etta ran her hands up Gwen's sides.

"This is a spectacular idea." Etta slipped her hands under Gwen's suit jacket, and Gwen felt them searing against the skin under her blouse. "That was the hottest thing I've ever seen in person."

"What was?" Gwen wasn't fishing for a compliment. She genuinely didn't know what Etta was talking about. Her brain had gone fuzzy again.

"That rebuttal. You shredded her arguments and I nearly overheated right there in the courtroom." Etta placed another kiss on Gwen's neck.

Gwen chuckled. "So, me being good at my job turned you on so much you had to come to my office and jump me?"

"What can I say? I have a competency kink. So sue me." Etta wrapped her arms tighter around Gwen and nuzzled under her jaw. "Actually, don't sue me."

Gwen looked at her in confusion. Etta was causing her brain to short-circuit, and she couldn't follow what Etta was saying.

"I don't want you to sue me because you would win. You gotta give me at least five years to have a fighting chance." Before Gwen could come up with an appropriate retort, Etta pressed their lips together one more time. This kiss lasted longer than the others and Gwen felt herself melting into Etta.

"You're right," Gwen said. "Not doing this is stupid." She desperately wanted Etta's fingers inside her.

"I knew you'd come around," Etta replied. She swept her hands up and rubbed her thumbs over Gwen's nipples through her clothing. Even the muted sensation had Gwen shuddering. She groaned, then pulled away.

"I'll come by your house tonight, but we are not having sex in my office." She pushed Etta away, and Etta stumbled back a step.

"You're sure?" Etta asked.

"Yes." Gwen took a deep breath. She stood up on slightly shaky legs and forced Etta back another step.

"I'll see you tonight?" Etta pressed.

Gwen leaned in for a quick kiss. "You'll see me tonight. We'll probably end up working late on the case, but I'll be there by eight."

A brilliant smile appeared on Etta's face. "Excellent," she said before backing up a few more steps.

Gwen smoothed her suit down. "Now shoo. I have work to do."

"All right. All right." Etta held her hands up in surrender. She opened the door and left Gwen's office.

As soon as she was gone, Gwen collapsed down into one of her guest chairs. This was a stupid, stupid idea, but she didn't care. Etta's touch was still rushing through her veins, and she didn't want to give that feeling up.

Her desk phone started ringing. She forced herself up and answered it. It was Brad inviting her to a congratulatory lunch. She didn't particularly want to go. She wanted to sit in her office and relive Etta's kisses, but that wasn't a legitimate reason to turn him down. She agreed to the lunch, then hung up. She had a few minutes to put herself back together before Brad made it down to her office. She was going to need all of them.

❖

Gwen settled into the seat across from Brad at a lunch counter down the street from the Dunleavy Byrd offices. They had already ordered at the counter and their lunches would be out soon.

"I heard you kicked ass and took names in the simulation this morning." Brad stretched his arms out along the back of the low booth.

"I certainly tried. We're meeting about it after lunch. We'll go over everything that went right and everything we can improve upon. Lindsay came up with a new interpretation of the case law that I didn't expect, so we'll have to figure out the best way to counter it. I'm not entirely happy with what I managed on the fly." Gwen frowned. She had come up with a response, but she didn't know if it was the best one, and for this case, she needed to be perfect.

She also needed to not be distracted by Etta and the promise of seeing her again that night. Normally, she'd call Grey to talk it over, but she already knew what Grey would say. Grey would tell her to stop. To not go to Etta's that night. To avoid Etta like the plague at work and never see her again socially. It was too risky, and she couldn't afford those sorts of risks right now.

Grey wouldn't understand how addictive Etta was. She was on her own.

"From what I hear, you don't have anything to worry about, but I'm sure you'll do better with some time to prepare." Brad smiled at the waitress as she placed his food in front of him. The waitress smiled back. Most of the time, Gwen forgot how charming Brad could be when he wanted to be. She had never been taken by that charm, but she understood how other people were. It was part of what made him so successful. "So, how's your application for that other job going?"

Considering where they were in Midtown, the entire lunch counter was probably crawling with lawyers. Gwen appreciated Brad's discretion. Her interest might be part of the public record, but most people wouldn't be keeping track of that. It would be much more gossip-worthy if they overheard her ambitions at lunch.

"On pause until after these arguments. The questionnaire is certainly thorough. Among many other things, I have to come up with percentages for how much time I've spent in state versus federal court. The amount of research that's going to take is almost overwhelming." Gwen shook her head. "And that's only one question."

"So, poach another associate from general litigation, shift your workload around, and focus on the application. I'll approve a temporary transfer," Brad said like it was no big deal. Gwen knew what he was talking about wouldn't be so easily accomplished. "Give more responsibility to Lindsay. Someone's going to need to take over once you're gone, and I'd rather we find someone in house than trying to recruit."

"And how am I going to explain to Lindsay why I'm suddenly giving her so much more responsibility?" Gwen asked.

"You already do more on the admin side than most of the other section heads. Tell her you want to be able to focus on the litigation instead of all of the bullshit you have to do for the firm. Tell her it's like a promotion."

"But without a bump in salary or title. I'm sure she'll love that." Gwen pursed her lips. Brad had an answer for everything, but that didn't mean they were good answers.

"Gwen, it's a way for her to prove herself. You'll be gone in six months, and then she'll have to do all of it anyway. That's assuming she can handle it now," Brad said. "And this way if she falls apart under the added responsibility, you'll be there to fix it before you hand it off to someone else. What you're doing is important. You don't have to do everything by yourself. Let me help you."

Gwen threw up her hands. "Fine. All right. I'll take the help. But I want Trevor from general litigation. I've had my eye on him for months. I just haven't had a reason to justify asking for a transfer."

"Done." Brad clapped his hands and then rubbed them together. "Now, I don't know about you, but I'm hungry."

"You're always hungry." Gwen gave him a look that said she knew what he was doing by trying to change the subject.

"That's true," Brad replied. He picked up his sandwich and took a bite. He held up a finger while he chewed indicating he had something else to say. "Oh, I saw a report yesterday, one of the ones I generally like to delegate. You need to do your yearly sexual harassment training. Just because the training was your idea doesn't make you exempt."

Gwen was positive her face turned bright red, but Brad didn't say anything about it. He looked invested in his sandwich.

"I'll do it today." Gwen swallowed uncomfortably.

❖

Etta paced nervously. It was just after eight and she hadn't heard from Gwen. Had Gwen changed her mind? Was she going to have to sit through another conversation about how what they were doing wasn't appropriate and why they shouldn't do it? She didn't have a great argument against that beyond how she felt when Gwen's arms were around her. Surely, that counted for something. She was about to call Gwen when she heard the knocking on her door. It only took her a second to open it and find Gwen on the other side.

"Parking down here is truly atrocious," Gwen said as she stepped inside. "I was tempted to take an Uber from my condo."

"Gwen." Etta broke into Gwen's monologue. "Shut up." She pushed the door closed and reached for Gwen, snagging her shirt and pulling her close. Then she covered Gwen's lips with her own.

Gwen wrapped her arms around Etta's shoulders, pulling her even closer. Somehow, knowing that they shouldn't be doing this made everything even hotter. Etta couldn't keep her hands off Gwen, letting them roam down her sides before she started to untuck Gwen's shirt. Gwen was still in her suit from that morning and Etta wanted nothing more than to strip it from her body. With nothing to stop her, she started to do exactly that.

First, she pushed Gwen's jacket off her shoulders, letting it fall to the ground. Then she started unbuttoning her shirt. It followed the jacket, landing on top of it. Gwen pressed closer and started to tug at Etta's T-shirt. It was nothing to pull it over her head and off.

"Bed. Now," Gwen gasped.

"There's a perfectly good couch right here," Etta replied. She'd be happy to go down on Gwen while Gwen sat on the couch. In fact, right that second, that was exactly what she wanted to do.

"Bed," Gwen reiterated, extracting herself from Etta's arms. She seemingly ignored Etta's complaining groan and walked into the bedroom. Etta had no choice but to follow her.

It only took Etta a few seconds to catch up, but by the time she did, Gwen already had her pants off. Etta groaned again, though for much better reasons this time. Gwen opened her arms and Etta slid into them. She was ecstatic that Gwen hadn't come up with any reasons why they shouldn't do this, and she fully intended to take advantage of Gwen's silence on the subject.

Etta unhooked Gwen's bra, then pushed her toward the bed. Seconds later, she climbed on top of Gwen. She was going to thoroughly enjoy herself that night. They would see what the next day brought when the sun came up.

CHAPTER FOURTEEN

Gwen slowly opened her eyes and took a deep breath. Etta was curled up against her back, and she stretched into her. Etta tightened her arms as if she were loath to let Gwen go.

"Are you leaving?" Etta whispered hoarsely.

"Eventually. Not yet, though." Gwen rolled over and wrapped an arm around Etta's waist before nuzzling against her. "I don't have anywhere to be today. Do you?"

"I thought I might go grocery shopping, but I never have groceries, so I can put it off until tomorrow." Etta nuzzled back and rubbed her legs against Gwen's.

"You should go buy food." Gwen exhaled contentedly. "You can't have takeout for every meal."

"Says you. I manage just fine." Etta closed her eyes and kissed Gwen's jaw.

"I'll go with you," Gwen offered. That couldn't possibly be a good idea, but she had already offered, and she didn't want to take it back.

"I guess that would be okay," Etta grumbled.

"It's that or I set up grocery delivery for you." Gwen trailed her fingers down Etta's spine.

"You say that like it's a threat." Etta took a deep breath and arched into Gwen's fingers.

"It is a threat. It would be all vegetables and distinctly lacking in Lucky Charms and Pop-Tarts." Gwen kissed Etta briefly. "I saw what you keep in your kitchen that night I cooked for you. I'm concerned about your health. It's amazing you don't have scurvy."

"Pop-Tarts have vitamin C," Etta replied.

Gwen chuckled. "You're purposefully missing my point."

Etta pushed on Gwen's shoulder to move her onto her back before straddling her hips. "Stop talking about food. Spend more time fucking me." She rolled her hips against Gwen's.

Gwen put her hands on Etta's thighs and skimmed them up to her hips. "You make a compelling case," she said, then she pulled Etta down to her where they could kiss. A quick movement later and Etta was on her back, Gwen braced above her. "I'll fuck you now, but then we're getting breakfast and going to the grocery store."

"Let's start with the first thing on your list. We can renegotiate the rest of it later." Etta hooked a leg over Gwen's hip and pulled her closer. At that point, Gwen forgot about groceries altogether.

❖

Etta walked down the aisle at the nearest grocery store, pushing a cart as Gwen walked beside her. As many times as Etta had tried to distract her, Gwen wouldn't be deterred from completing this errand.

"You're judging me." Etta looked over at Gwen and then down at her cart full of processed foods.

"I'm not judging you." Gwen suppressed a laugh.

"You are. I can feel it." Despite her words, Etta couldn't stop herself from smiling. She hadn't expected this, Gwen walking beside her through a grocery store as if she didn't have a care in the world. Well, other than her general concern for Etta's health.

"Surely, there is at least one vegetable that you like," Gwen said as she looked down at the cart in despair.

"Of course there are vegetables that I like. I just suck at cooking them. I suck at cooking most things." It was something she had known about herself for most of her adult life.

"But you make such good martinis. How can you not cook?" Gwen lamented.

"I'm very good at making cocktails and I'm a decent baker. Sometimes, I even stress bake. I'm more than capable of following a recipe. I'm a terrible cook. Everything either comes out too salty or not salty enough. I burn things. I've never set a kitchen on fire, but I've come way too close for comfort. This is a thing I've accepted about myself. So, Pop-Tarts and takeout." Etta grabbed a package of instant rice and added it to her cart.

"All right. I'll stop pestering you." Gwen brushed her hand against the small of Etta's back.

"Thank you." Etta wanted to steal a kiss, but she had a feeling they weren't at that point.

"But you should come over tonight and let me feed you something that isn't overly processed," Gwen offered.

"That wasn't me angling for a dinner invitation," Etta said. She pushed the cart farther down the aisle.

"I didn't think it was, but I'm extending one anyway." Gwen shook her head, though it seemed in affectionate exasperation rather than real annoyance.

"Let me bring drinks and I'll come for dinner," Etta replied.

"All right." Gwen nodded like they had just finished an important negotiation and she had come out on top. "I do have to get some work done first, so I'm going to leave you at your house once we get back there."

"I thought the firm discouraged people from bringing work home?" Etta asked. She definitely remembered that from her orientation.

"It discourages you from bringing work home. I have enough leeway to do whatever I want. Except get out of the annual sexual harassment training, apparently." Gwen smiled ruefully.

"Ironic."

"Don't remind me." Gwen took a deep breath. "Come on. Let's finish up here. The sooner I get home, the sooner I can get to work, and the sooner I can be finished with work."

"And then you can make sure I don't die from scurvy," Etta added on. She liked spending time with Gwen like this. She hoped that they could do it more often.

❖

Etta knocked on Gwen's door, surprised when it opened easily under her fingers. She pushed it open the rest of the way and stepped inside.

"Hello?" she called out as she looked for Gwen.

Gwen appeared from the hallway that led to the bedrooms. "Hello."

She took her reading glasses off as she walked. She was still wearing the yoga pants and T-shirt Etta had loaned her that morning, which Etta thought looked particularly good on her. She leaned in for a kiss, which started short but then lingered. Eventually, they managed to pull away from each other.

"You left your door open," Etta pointed out, though Gwen had to have known what she'd done. She shifted her grip on the bottle in her hand.

"There's only one other person on this floor, and the doorman calls me before he lets anyone up." Gwen motioned toward the door. "I'm putting some last touches on a brief that needs to be finished by Monday. It's been languishing. Oral arguments for the Fletcher case have taken precedence, but this still needs to get finished."

"Do you work all the time?" Etta asked.

"No." Gwen smiled and leaned in for another quick kiss. "Sometimes, I take pity on young people and cook them dinner, thus ensuring that they don't get scurvy."

"Are you cooking meals for many young people?"

"Yes. My son." Gwen looked at Etta pointedly.

"Oh, ouch." Etta put her hands over her heart, mimicking a mortal wound. "Please tell me I don't remind you of your son."

Gwen laughed. "Not even a little." She pulled Etta closer and nuzzled against her before placing a kiss on the side of her neck.

Etta moaned but stepped away. "If you keep doing that, we won't ever eat."

"And thus, you'll perish from malnutrition. I can take a hint."

Gwen took Etta's hand. "Come into the kitchen with me while I decide what we're going to have tonight."

Etta followed Gwen across the condo and into the kitchen. Once she got there, she put the bottle she was still carrying down on the center island. "You mean you don't have some sort of elaborate four-course meal planned out?"

"I do not. What's in the bottle?" It didn't have a label on it, so Gwen had no way to know.

"You requested that I bring drinks. Those are the drinks." Etta smiled. "I assumed you had a shaker, but if you don't, stirring them won't be too much of a travesty."

"The shaker is on the bar cart." Gwen pointed. "You can help yourself to ice from the refrigerator. Glasses?"

"Coupes if you have them. Something short if you don't." She wasn't fussy about what they drank out of.

Gwen went over to a far cabinet, opened it, and pulled out two coupes, which she carried over to the center island. "Acceptable?"

"You're the only person I know who could pull those out of thin air without knowing you'd need them first." Etta turned, walked over to the bar cart, and grabbed the shaker.

"I throw a lot of dinner parties," Gwen said. "And it pays to be prepared."

"If you say so." Etta moved through Gwen's kitchen getting everything she needed to chill the drinks. She had already mixed them. All they needed was ice.

"So, what are we drinking?" Gwen nodded toward the shaker in Etta's hand.

"Bee's Knees," Etta said. She shook the cocktails, then poured them into the two glasses. "I know you like gin, but they're more interesting than a martini. Also, martinis aren't really my thing. So, gin, lemon, and honey syrup. Sweet, but hopefully not cloying." She pushed one of the glasses in Gwen's direction. "Cheers."

They touched their glasses together and Gwen took a testing sip. "All right, you can stay." She smiled as she drank more of the cocktail.

"Well, I've got to pay you back for the dinner somehow," Etta said.

"You don't, but I'm not going to stop you from bringing me more of these." Gwen put her drink down.

"Oh, I'll bring something different next time," Etta replied automatically. Then she paused. Would there be a next time? She hadn't meant to assume there would be. She looked at Gwen to see how she was reacting.

Gwen also looked frozen in place, but she recovered before Etta did. Deliberately, she said, "I look forward to it," and Etta let out a relieved breath.

"Yeah. Me too." She managed a tentative smile.

"So, dinner?" Gwen asked after she took another sip of her drink. "Do you have any requests?"

"I'm not big on broccoli, but other than that, I'm good," Etta said.

"No broccoli. I think I can manage that." Gwen smiled as she opened the refrigerator.

Etta put her drink down and walked over to where Gwen was staring at the contents of her refrigerator. She wrapped her arms around Gwen from behind and hugged her. "Thank you for having me over."

Gwen placed her hands on top of Etta's. "You're welcome here whenever you'd like." She squeezed Etta's hands. "But you need to stop distracting me or we'll never eat."

"Fine. Fine." Etta let go of Gwen and resumed her place by the island. "Do your magic. I'm getting hungry anyway."

CHAPTER FIFTEEN

It was Wednesday. Wednesday meant oral arguments for the Fletcher case. Wednesday meant getting up early and getting to the office where Gwen could do her last-minute prep before she went to the Supreme Court building. They were in the afternoon spot and Gwen hated it. She'd much rather go first thing in the morning and get it over with. But it was what it was. She didn't control the schedule. It was better to use her energy on the things she could control. She was preparing to leave her condo when the doorman called her cell phone.

She answered and told him to let Etta up. She had no idea why Etta was there, and she hoped that whatever she wanted wouldn't take long. As much as she liked spending time with Etta, she needed to get to work. She went ahead and opened her door, standing by it while the elevator climbed.

As the doors opened, Gwen couldn't stop herself from smiling despite the inconvenience. Etta walked out of the elevator and straight to Gwen.

"I know you don't have much time, but I brought you breakfast." Etta held up a foil-wrapped packet that Gwen knew contained Pop-Tarts. She laughed at the absurdity.

"Don't laugh. They're strawberry." Despite her words, Etta was laughing too.

"I've already had breakfast, but I appreciate the sentiment." As soon as Etta was close enough, Gwen leaned in for a kiss.

"Then you can have them for a snack later." Etta held out the packet. Gwen had no choice but to take it, and she did so with good humor.

"I'll put them in my bag. Now, I know you didn't come up here to bring me breakfast." Gwen led Etta into her condo.

"Oh, but I did. I absolutely did." Etta reached for Gwen's free hand. "And I wanted to see you before your arguments today. I thought you'd prefer that I do it here than find an excuse to come by your office."

"Thinking ahead," Gwen replied.

"Mm-hmm." Etta stepped closer until she could wrap her arms around Gwen. She tilted her head for another kiss, which Gwen happily gave her. "I wanted to wish you luck. And tell you to kick ass."

"Thank you." Gwen smiled. She let Etta go. "For the offer of luck. And I am absolutely going to kick ass." Gwen had no doubts about that. She was ready. She was going to walk into the courtroom and do everything she could to ensure that her clients won. She was determined that opposing counsel wouldn't know what hit them.

"Has anyone ever told you you're sexy when you're being egotistical?" Etta asked.

"You would be the first," Gwen replied.

"Well, just so you know, the entire cadre of summer associates is going to be there cheering you on. Metaphorically speaking. I think they frown on actual cheering in the courtroom," Etta said.

"I know. Having you all come was my idea," Gwen said. "I thought after the show in the moot courtroom, the four of you might like to see the real thing. I know you're not interested in appellate law, but that doesn't mean that one of them isn't."

"So, it'll be educational, is what you're saying. And it isn't at all about how I nearly jumped you the last time I saw you eviscerate someone in court?"

"It is not," Gwen said emphatically. "Though if you wanted to repeat the outcome tonight, I wouldn't turn you away."

"Noted."

"Now, I need to get to work, and you need to get to work."

Gwen leaned in for one last kiss. "I'll see you after arguments are finished. Enjoy reviewing contracts all morning."

"Don't remind me. I've got another week and a half of it before they move me to Intellectual Property for three weeks." Etta turned and opened the door before walking back into the hallway.

Gwen picked up her bag and followed Etta outside. She locked her door and headed toward the elevator.

"Maybe they'll let you help with a trademark application. Otherwise, IP is more contracts," Gwen said.

Etta groaned as she stepped into the elevator. "I hate this summer."

"If you got a position with Dunleavy Byrd, I assume your grades are spectacular. You could have done anything you wanted with this summer. Why did you decide to do this?" Gwen asked. It didn't make sense to her.

"My mom wanted me to. Like, really, really wanted me to. And it's hard to turn down the salary when you're eking by on scholarships," Etta said.

"Well, at least you've learned that you don't want to go into corporate law. Maybe litigation will be more appealing." Gwen brushed her fingers over the back of Etta's hand.

"I hope so." Etta tangled her fingers with Gwen's, squeezed them, and then let go. The elevator doors opened, and they both stepped out.

Gwen waved at the doorman, then turned to Etta. "My car's in the parking deck, and I'm assuming you've parked on the street."

"Yup," Etta replied. She looked over her shoulder toward the doors that led to the street before turning back to Gwen. "Like I said, go kick ass. I'm going to enjoy watching it."

"I will." Gwen smiled ruthlessly. Gwen wanted to kiss Etta goodbye, but that seemed risky now that they were at street level and anyone could walk in the building's front doors. "I'll see you later."

"Count on it." With a last look, Etta turned around and headed outside.

Gwen watched her go. With a shake of her head to reset herself, she headed to the parking garage. Maybe she'd get Etta a parking pass. That was something to think about later, though. For now, she had a case to go win.

❖

Etta settled into her seat in the supreme court gallery and waited for the show to start. Gwen was sitting in the first row with Lindsay—Etta had finally learned her name—sitting next to her. They had their heads bowed together, probably discussing last-minute strategy.

It was only a short wait before the marshal called the court to order. Everyone stood as the justices entered the courtroom and took their seats on the bench. Somehow, the nine of them were more imposing than the fake justices had been in the moot courtroom. They carried a gravitas that the people pretending to be them hadn't. Before Etta could figure out why, the marshal directed them all to be seated again.

Almost before everyone in the gallery had taken their seats, the case was called, and Gwen stood up and walked to the appellant's table. As her name and the name of the opposing counsel were announced, she placed her binder on the podium.

"Ms. Strickland, you can proceed when ready."

"Thank you, Mr. Chief Justice." Gwen's voice cut through the small amount of chatter going on and everyone quieted. Once she had the justices' attention, she introduced herself and began her argument. Etta realized quickly that she had heard almost all of it before. This time, Gwen managed two and a half minutes before the justices started interrupting her with questions.

Instead of focusing on what Gwen had to say, Etta tried to picture Gwen up on the bench, asking probing questions to nervous attorneys. It wasn't hard to do. Gwen's interest was part of the public record, and if anyone was paying attention to the list of interested parties, it was the nine men and women sitting at the front of the courtroom. They had to know that Gwen was vying to join their ranks.

If they did know, Etta couldn't tell. Clearly, most of the justices had made their minds up after reading the briefs, and their questions seemed to be attempts to get their fellows to agree with them, but Gwen answered the questions either way. She argued forcefully. She argued confidently.

Etta couldn't fault Gwen for her ambitions. Gwen looked utterly at home arguing before the court. Becoming a member of the court was so clearly the next step in her career as to be an almost forgone conclusion. If their relationship made accomplishing that harder, then the two of them would just have to be very, very discreet.

Etta had a feeling that thinking about sex while in the supreme court gallery wasn't something she should do, but she couldn't stop herself. She wanted to take Gwen, pin her down somewhere, and do dirty, dirty things to her. She wanted to take Gwen apart and leave her a sweaty, shaking mess, begging Etta for release.

Someone in the gallery cleared their throat and pulled Etta out of her fantasies. She needed to work on her focus. Someone was bound to ask her how the arguments had gone. She needed to pay attention to enough of them to be able to answer that question.

Gwen wrapped up her arguments and returned to the appellant's table.

❖

Gwen stepped out of the courthouse doors and took what felt like the first deep breath she had taken in the last two hours. The hearing was over. She had done everything she could. It was up to the justices now. By her count, based on their questions, she had at least three of them convinced. She needed two more to reach her five-justice majority. At this point, it was out of her hands.

Lindsay clapped her on the back as she came up from behind her. "You just crushed that."

"We'll see." Gwen couldn't help but be cautious. It would be a while before the decision got released.

"Even if we don't win, that argument was one of the best you've ever given," Lindsay said. "You did everything you could."

"Thank you." Unlike the argument in the moot courtroom, which left her feeling energized, right now, she felt wrung out. She had a few things she needed to wrap up at the office, but once she did that, she was taking the rest of the day off. She'd probably only end up leaving a few minutes early, but she'd do her best. Her brain wasn't going to be useful for much anyway.

Her phone had been off while she was in the courtroom. Now, she turned it on. Once it buzzed back to life, she saw a text from Etta. The message was simple: *My place or yours?*

❖

Gwen stepped into Etta's house and pulled Etta into her arms. "I'm exhausted. But if you feed me, I might turn into a responsive human again."

"Adrenaline crash?" Etta asked. She nuzzled against Gwen's neck and left a kiss there.

"Mm-hmm." Gwen pulled Etta even closer.

"What happened to the Pop-Tarts I gave you?" Etta pulled back far enough to look Gwen in the face.

"I ate them back at the firm. You should have seen Sam's face when I walked back to my office with them. They worked for about an hour. Then there was a section meeting that I forgot about. We spent another hour rehashing everything that happened during the arguments. My brain is fried."

"You know I don't cook, right?" Etta let go of Gwen and guided her down onto the couch.

"But you probably have more takeout menus than I do, because there's no way I'm cooking either." Now that she was sitting down, Gwen closed her eyes.

"That seems likely. Give me a second and I'll get them." Gwen heard Etta leave the room and then come back. The couch dipped as Etta sat next to her. "Okay, you have to open your eyes to decide on something, but after that you can take a nap."

"Mmm." Gwen opened her eyes and held out her hand for the

menus. "You've only been here for two weeks. How do you have eighteen takeout menus already?"

Etta shrugged. "It's my superpower."

"Takeout is your superpower?" Gwen flipped through the menus until she came to one that sounded good. She read through it until she found something she liked.

"Finding good takeout is my superpower. Tell me what you want, and I'll order it," Etta offered.

"The lamb vindaloo. Spicy, but not excessively spicy. That should wake me up." Gwen handed the menu back.

"Got it." Etta grabbed her phone and placed their orders. She didn't need to look at the menu. She already had a regular thing that she ate.

"Now, take your shoes off and get some sleep. I have plans for you later, and I need you to be conscious for them." Etta gently pushed Gwen until she was lying down on the couch, her legs stretched across Etta's lap.

"I like that sound of that." Gwen shifted to get more comfortable.

"You'll like the reality better." Etta pulled Gwen's shoes off.

Gwen pushed deeper into the couch. She couldn't remember a time when she had felt so taken care of. Sleep wasn't far away.

CHAPTER SIXTEEN

Etta shifted on Gwen's couch and flipped the page in the book she was reading. It was a Wednesday night in the middle of June and she and Gwen had developed a routine. Weekends, they lounged around Etta's house, but on Wednesdays, Gwen cooked dinner at her condo. She said it was preventive healthcare to stop Etta from dying from malnutrition.

Etta didn't have time to read during the school year, and the firm's moratorium against working from home meant that she didn't have much to do with her nights after the inevitable receptions. It seemed like every section at the firm either had a lunch or a dinner or a reception for them. The attention was flattering, but also overwhelming. She was much happier on Gwen's couch.

She was partway through the chapter she was reading when Gwen appeared at the end of the hallway. Her reading glasses were perched on the top of her head, and she had a binder in one hand.

Etta moved around so Gwen could sit next to her, and Gwen sank into the cushions with a groan.

"What's up?" Etta asked as Gwen put her socked feet up on the coffee table. She closed her eyes and held the binder out to Etta. Etta plucked it from her hand and opened it to see what was inside.

"I've narrowed it down to two, but I can't decide which one is better." Gwen opened her eyes back up, looking at Etta pleadingly. "I don't suppose you'd like to decide?"

"What am I deciding?" Etta looked at the first page in the binder with greater interest. It had a supreme court heading on the top of it. She flipped to the second page where the argument actually started.

"I need to submit a writing sample with my application. It turns out that I've written quite a lot over an eighteen-year career. I cut it down to supreme court briefs that I've written in the last two years. I've reread all of them. Those are the best two." Gwen rubbed her eyes.

"And you want me to...?" Etta trailed off. Gwen couldn't be asking her what she thought she was asking her.

"Pick one," Gwen said, like the decision wasn't one of the most important in her career.

"Pick one? Shouldn't someone at the firm do this? Someone who isn't still a law student?" It didn't make sense to Etta that Gwen would ask her of all people to do this for her.

"Brad doesn't have time. Everyone in the appellate section has already read them, and I'm trying to keep as much of this away from work as I can. You have fresh eyes, and you won't feel the need to flatter me. I already know they're good. I could use either of them. I just want to know which one is better," Gwen said. "I trust you to tell me that."

"Well, okay," Etta said. "Can I write on these?" She nodded toward the papers in the binder.

"Pencil, pen, or highlighter?" Gwen put her feet back on the floor and stood up.

"Pencil." Etta looked up at Gwen. She was still amazed that Gwen trusted her to do this, but she would approach it with the seriousness it deserved.

"Thank you." Gwen leaned down and placed a kiss on Etta's lips before she disappeared down the hallway to her home office. She came back a minute later with a pencil and handed it over.

"You're lucky I like you a whole lot. I wouldn't spend my free time reading supreme court briefs for just anyone," Etta said as she took the pencil. "Now, go away while I read." She made a shooing motion with her hands directing Gwen back to her office. Once Gwen was gone, she closed her eyes and shifted into the proper mindset for her task. She needed to take it much more seriously than she had been taking her book. She tried not to think about how part of Gwen's supreme court bid was literally in her hands.

❖

"You should use the first one. *Banks v. Draper Corp*," Etta said as she walked into Gwen's office. Gwen looked up from her computer and spun her chair to face the door.

"Why that one?" Gwen was willing to use either of the briefs, but she wanted to hear Etta's reasoning. She was curious about why Etta would pick one over the other.

"The other one's too technical," Etta said. "Don't get me wrong, it's still excellent, but I think the people on the commission might get lost in the weeds. They're not all as smart as you." Etta smiled mischievously as she approached Gwen. She held out the binder, which Gwen took and set aside. Then she leaned in and braced her hands on the arms of Gwen's chair.

Gwen closed her eyes at the closeness. She took a shuddering breath, then opened her eyes again. Somehow, Etta was even closer.

With a quick movement, Etta straddled Gwen's lap. "I know you won't let me fuck you in your office at work, but I'm hoping the rules might be different for this office."

Gwen put her hands on Etta's thighs, rubbing them against the stretchy yoga pants as Etta leaned in and kissed her. Gwen let herself get lost in the kiss, bringing her hands up over Etta's hips and under her shirt until she could touch skin.

"I don't understand your obsession with having sex in my office," Gwen said when they parted slightly. She was breathing heavily, and she was inclined to do whatever Etta wanted.

"Let me have my power fantasy," Etta replied as she brushed her nose against Gwen's.

Gwen did love to indulge Etta's fantasies. They always ended up enjoyable for both of them.

"Mmm." Gwen kissed Etta again. "If that's what you want,

shouldn't you be on your knees?" Gwen pressed down on Etta's hips to guide her to the ground, her look of imperiousness growing as Etta moaned.

"I might start on my knees, but that's not how we're going to end this night." Etta slid onto the floor, scratching her fingers over Gwen's thighs.

"Oh?" Gwen shuddered at the way Etta was touching her. She didn't really care how they ended the night. She would do whatever Etta wanted.

"Nope. I fully intend on stealing your strap-on and bending you over this desk," Etta said as she kissed the inside of Gwen's thigh. "After you make me come."

Gwen moaned. Etta's words made her thoughts go fuzzy.

"But I'm going to go down on you first, so we should get rid of these pants." Etta reached for the waistband of Gwen's lounge pants. She hooked her fingers into them and started tugging. "Enjoy being in charge while it lasts."

❖

It was July Fourth and even though it was only mid-morning, the temperature outside was somewhere above sweltering. Gwen was happy to be lounging in bed at her condo with Etta for their extended weekend. She thought they might watch the fireworks later from her balcony, but that was for after it got dark. For now, she was content to let Etta doze beside her in the bed while she indulged in some non-work-related reading.

"Mom?" Christian's voice called out through the condo, the sound of the door closing behind him a sharp staccato. Gwen's eyes went wide. Christian was supposed to be spending the summer in Cartersville doing an internship. She tried to think whether he had told her he was coming to town, but she couldn't think of any sort of communication to that effect.

She looked over at Etta, who was still asleep beside her. Luckily, they were both dressed because she could hear Christian's footsteps coming down the hallway. She knew she wouldn't have enough time to make it out of bed to intercept him before he knocked on the bedroom door.

She rubbed a hand against Etta's back. "You need to wake up now."

"Hmm?" Etta rolled over and wrapped an arm around Gwen's hips.

"My son is here. I thought you might want to be awake." Gwen said softly.

"What?" Etta's eyes flew open, and she pushed herself upright.

There was a tap on the door, and "Mom?" filtered through it.

Gwen got out of bed and pulled on a robe before going over to open the bedroom door.

"Hello, darling." Gwen stepped into the hallway and closed the bedroom door behind herself, but not before Christian obviously saw Etta. She leaned in and kissed his cheek before breezing past him and toward the condo's main room.

"Mom?" Christian paused and looked at the door before turning and following her. "What's going on?"

"What do you think is going on?" Gwen asked in return. Better not to assume he knew more than he did and shock him unnecessarily.

"I think I just found you in bed with another woman," Christian replied, his voice going up in pitch at the end of the statement.

"That would be an accurate statement. Her name is Etta, and she's a friend. I won't have you be rude to her." She swept into the kitchen and opened the refrigerator. "Would you like breakfast?"

"Are we not going to talk about the fact that I found you in bed with someone? With a woman?" Christian flung a hand back toward the hallway to the bedroom.

Gwen gave Christian a deadpan stare. "Christian, I know I didn't raise you to have a problem with gay people. And I've been bisexual since before you were born."

"You have?" Christian looked at her agog.

"Yes. I'm not quite sure how you've missed that." She took out the carton of eggs and placed it on the counter.

"Well, you were with Dad, and I assumed. I mean, I assumed you went on dates sometimes without telling me, but I didn't have any reason to think they might be with women. Does Dad know?" Christian asked.

"Of course he knows. He knew when we started dating. Christian, I'm sorry if you're only now figuring it out, but it's never particularly been a secret. You've gone to Pride almost every year since you were a baby." Gwen reached out and put a hand on his arm. "I'm sorry I shocked you. Now, what are you doing in town? I thought you wanted to stay in Cartersville this summer."

"It's a long weekend. I thought I'd come see you. And some friends and I are going to see a band we like tonight. But, uh, I can go hang out with them for the rest of the day. I didn't mean to interrupt anything." Christian looked down the hallway and then back at Gwen.

"The only thing you interrupted was Etta's morning nap." Gwen took a moment to pull out a large bowl, a whisk, and a frying pan. "Now, let me make you breakfast and then you can escape this mortifying experience and be with your friends."

"You don't have to do that," Christian said.

"Have you had breakfast?" Gwen asked. She looked at Christian intently.

"No." Christian seemed resigned to the fact that he would have to stay long enough to eat.

"Exactly. Now, crack some eggs for me while I get the bacon started." Gwen left the eggs to Christian. She hadn't intended to introduce Etta to her son, but unless Etta spent the next hour hiding, there was no getting around it now.

❖

Etta emerged from the bedroom five minutes later. She looked around in trepidation, as if someone might have set a trap for her in the middle of Gwen's condo. She had changed into yoga pants and a T-shirt, figuring that staying in her night clothes wasn't the best move when she was about to meet Gwen's son.

Even though she and Gwen had been involved for a few

months, she had never seriously considered meeting Christian. He was a shadowy figure that existed outside of the haven they had constructed for themselves. Still, it seemed like now she wasn't going to have a choice. She could hear Gwen and Christian talking, so he hadn't run away yet. She wondered if they would notice if she slipped out the front door.

Probably.

There was nothing to do for it but to go into the kitchen and confront the situation head-on.

Etta emerged from the hallway and into the living room. She could see Gwen at the stove cooking something in a frying pan. Christian stood next to her looking as awkward as Etta felt. He was taller than his mother, though not by much. Their blond hair seemed to be the only thing they had in common. If she had seen them on the street, she wasn't sure she would have pegged them as mother and child.

"Oh, Etta, you're up." Gwen smiled at her, but it was a tight smile. It seemed like this situation was getting to Gwen as well. "I'm making eggs. Would you like some?"

"Uh, scrambled would be good." Etta looked between Gwen and Christian. Well, they couldn't all stand there looking awkwardly at each other all day. Someone needed to say something, and it looked like it was going to be her.

"Hi," Etta said as she walked toward them. She held out her hand. "I'm Etta."

Christian didn't particularly look like he wanted to shake her hand, but it appeared that he was too polite to refuse. "Christian." He took her hand and shook it.

"It's nice to meet you. Gwen has mentioned you." That was at least somewhat true. Gwen hadn't said much about him, but she didn't pretend that he didn't exist either.

"That's, uh, nice," Christian echoed. Then he looked between Etta and his mom as though he was looking for the right thing to say. Etta didn't know what to say either. She wondered if she looked as young to Gwen as Christian looked to her. "You know what, Mom, I should probably take off. I don't want to interrupt whatever you've got going on here."

Christian stepped away from the counter and toward the door.

"You're not interrupting," Gwen said as she reached out to take his hand. Christian allowed the touch for a minute before pulling away.

"It's cool. I can meet up with my friends. They wanted to hit a record store that looked interesting." Christian shifted his weight from one foot to the other. "You guys should enjoy the eggs, though." Without looking back or giving Gwen time to respond, Christian hurried out of the condo. Etta watched Gwen's growing concern as the door closed.

"So, that was Christian," Etta said as she looked at the closed door. "He seemed nice, I guess." Not that she'd had much time to come to any sort of conclusion about him.

"He's normally a bit more sociable." Gwen shrugged helplessly before she focused on the eggs again.

"Er, is it okay that I met him?" Etta asked. The vibe in the room was weird and Etta didn't like that.

"Of course. I just wish I had more time to prepare both of you." Gwen shook her head like she was trying to shake off the last few minutes. Etta went over to her and took the spatula she was using out of her hands.

"Hey. Everything's fine. I met Christian. Christian met me. The world didn't end. It'll be okay." Etta grasped Gwen's hands and squeezed them. "Maybe it wasn't the best of circumstances, but everything is okay."

"Right." Gwen paused. "You're right." She squeezed Etta's hands back. "Thank you for reminding me." Gwen leaned in for a quick kiss then pulled away. "Now, give me back the spatula before the eggs burn."

"Yes, ma'am," Etta said as she laughed. Leave it to Gwen to be concerned about the eggs right now. Still, as the person who would be eating the eggs, she was happy to let Gwen focus on them.

❖

"To surviving IP." Gwen raised her glass and Etta clinked her glass against it.

"Thank God," Etta said before she took a sip of her margarita. The tequila burned pleasantly against the back of her tongue. They were sitting on Etta's porch swing rocking slowly back and forth, a pitcher of margaritas sitting within easy reach on a side table. The heat had abated as the sun had set. "Who knew filling out trademark applications was as boring as reviewing contracts?"

Gwen kept her silence.

Etta twisted to look up at her. "You did. You don't even have to say anything. I know you did." Etta resettled back against Gwen.

"I'm sorry. I'm sure you'll find something you enjoy eventually." Gwen kissed Etta's temple. "What do they have you doing on Monday?"

"Litigation. I'll wrap up my summer there." Etta stretched her legs out.

"I hope you like legal research." Gwen took a sip of her drink.

"I do, actually. Or I like it better than I do reviewing contracts. I had an excellent teacher," Etta said.

"Good. Maybe you'll finally enjoy yourself." Gwen gave the swing a little push.

"I've been enjoying myself," Etta objected. "Some of the lunches have been excellent. The other summer associates aren't all that bad. And the weekends can't be beat." She twisted around again and stole a kiss.

"I'm glad I could help make your summer worthwhile." Gwen ran her fingers up the outside of Etta's arm.

"Even if I'm constantly dragging you out to EAV?" Etta asked.

"I like it out here. It's like an escape from reality." Gwen took another sip of her drink. EAV was eclectic, but it was far enough removed from the city to feel like a real neighborhood without turning into a soulless suburb.

"But you won't be looking for any real estate in the area," Etta said.

"I like my condo. Why would I want to move?" Midtown suited her and her lifestyle.

"I'm not saying you do, or you should. It was just an observation." Etta rubbed her hand down Gwen's thigh and Gwen relaxed again. "You're staying the night?" Etta asked.

"If you'll have me." It was a conversation they had every weekend. Gwen practically moved into Etta's house over the weekends, but she still liked to make sure she was welcome.

"Have I ever kicked you out?"

"Not yet," Gwen said. "You might change your mind though."

"You're welcome here whenever you'd like, up to July thirtieth when I'm moving out." Etta snuggled further into Gwen's arms.

"What are your plans for the two weeks between then and when classes start?" Gwen tried to keep her voice light. She didn't know what was going to happen when Etta moved back to Cartersville and school started again, but she knew she didn't want whatever they were doing to end.

"I don't have any." Etta tangled the fingers of her free hand with Gwen's. "Errands to get ready for my last year, I guess."

"Let me find a beach for us to lie on." It was an impulsive offer, but Gwen didn't want to take it back. Spending a week someplace tropical with Etta sounded like heaven. "You won't be working for the firm anymore. We won't have to worry about keeping things so quiet."

Etta extracted herself from Gwen's arms and turned around to look at her. "Where would this beach be?"

"I've enjoyed Antigua in the past." She hadn't been in years, but she had a feeling the beaches hadn't changed that much.

"Antigua?" Etta sputtered after nearly having choked on her drink. "No. I'm not letting you sweep me off to a Caribbean island at the last minute. It would cost you a small fortune."

"It would be worth it."

"No."

"So, where can I take you?"

Etta rubbed her forehead. "Think domestic. And not Hawaii."

"I suppose I can work with that," Gwen said laughing. "We'll save Bali for Christmas."

"You are absolutely not taking me to Bali for Christmas." Etta's eyes went wide.

"I'll ask you about it again in October. You might change your mind by then." Gwen leaned in and stole a kiss.

"You're being ridiculous. I'm not going to change my mind," Etta said emphatically. "Bali." She leaned back against Gwen.

"Indonesia's beautiful," Gwen whispered in Etta's ear.

"Stop." Etta laughed, though it sounded like she was trying hard not to.

"Have you ever been to Southeast Asia?" Now Gwen was teasing her. Though she was seriously considering how much time she could get off from the firm at Christmas.

"That's it," Etta said as she stood up. "We're going inside, and I'm going to find something else we can do with your mouth that doesn't involve suggestions we vacation on other continents." She reached for Gwen's hand and tugged her up as well. Gwen nearly spilled her drink, but she didn't care. This was the most fun she had experienced in years, and she didn't want it to end. She saw no reason why it should.

Chapter Seventeen

Etta smiled as she took a sip of her mimosa. Sunday morning brunches were the only thing she let Gwen pay for while they were together, and she was happy to indulge in the decadence of the champagne before noon, and French toast slices drowned in rosemary maple syrup. They didn't often venture far from Etta's house on the weekends, but today they were up in Decatur at a restaurant that had just opened the weekend before. How Gwen had managed to get a reservation so quickly baffled Etta, but she suspected it might be one of the benefits of living in a building with a concierge. Maybe she shouldn't have dismissed that when she was first looking at places in the city.

"Where did you go?" Gwen asked as she tapped Etta's calf with her foot to get her attention.

"Hmm?" Etta replied, looking up at Gwen.

"You zoned out on me." Gwen tilted her head to the side slightly.

"Oh, I was thinking about the benefits of having a concierge in your building. I wouldn't want to live somewhere with one, but yours is very useful."

Etta reached her hand out for Gwen to take, and Gwen tangled their fingers together on top of the table.

"I'm glad this relationship benefits you in some way." Gwen looked at Etta with good humor.

Etta blinked. It was the first time she had heard Gwen refer to what they were doing as a relationship, and it made her pause. It left her with questions. "Is this a relationship?" She squeezed Gwen's fingers tighter.

"I…"

She watched as Gwen swallowed.

"I guess I just assumed—do you want it to be a relationship?"

Etta tried to think back to a time when she had seen Gwen be nervous, but she couldn't come up with one. She looked nervous now.

"Uh." Etta took a deep breath. She wanted to make sure she said the right thing, but the only thing she really wanted to do was launch herself across the table and kiss Gwen until neither of them could breathe. Instead, she went for a more sedate, "Yeah. I think I'd like that." Still, she couldn't stop smiling.

Gwen smiled back.

Etta tugged on Gwen's fingers until she had pulled them close enough where she could place a kiss on the back of them.

"Does this mean I can take you to Bali for Christmas now?" Gwen asked.

"No." Etta laughed. "We are not going to Bali for Christmas. My mom would murder me."

"You're no fun." Gwen shook her head in mock disappointment.

"I'm a ton of fun, but only in the contiguous forty-eight states." Etta gave Gwen a look that said she wasn't going to change her mind on that any time soon.

Gwen sighed as if to say that Etta was the one being unreasonable.

"Finish your omelet and let's get out of here. We can have significantly more fun back at my house," Etta said.

Gwen rolled her eyes. "Whatever you say, dear."

"Don't you start." Etta narrowed her eyes and pointed at Gwen.

Gwen laughed and before she knew it, Etta started laughing too.

❖

Gwen looked down at the thick envelope in her hand, weighing it. She double-checked the address. It was correct. As soon as she put it in the mail, it would be on its way to the commission.

"Gwen, if you ever want it to get there, you have to put it in the mail. I know it's important, but you can trust the post office." Etta wrapped an arm around Gwen's waist. "Let it go."

Gwen nodded. "I know." She stepped into the post office from the street and got in line. She wanted to send the packet return receipt. She was going to make sure it got to where it needed to be.

It was all there. The application. The writing sample. Both of the forms she needed to sign. Her picture. She had already emailed it all in, but the Commission required a hard copy as well.

Gwen spoke briefly to the woman behind that counter, then paid for her postage. Once that was finished, the woman whisked it away, putting it with a stack of other mail. Gwen looked at the envelope one last time before Etta pulled her away and out of the building.

❖

Gwen looked up as the door to her office opened. She wasn't expecting anyone, but she wasn't surprised to see Brad stepping inside. There weren't many people who could walk into her office unannounced, but he was on that short list.

"Gwen, I need you to come up to my office." Brad looked dour, and it set Gwen on edge.

"All right." She stood up from her desk and joined Brad at the door. "You know you could have just called."

Brad gave her another serious look and started walking toward the elevator. His office was a floor up, and he didn't seem inclined to say anything. With each step they took, Gwen got more anxious. She started going through scenarios in her head. If someone had died, they would have told her in her office. If she was about to be arrested for some unknown crime, they would have done that in her office as well. There was no scenario in which Brad wordlessly leading her to his office had a positive outcome, but she couldn't think of why they might be going there.

Brad opened his office door for Gwen and allowed her to go into the office before him. As she did, she saw Marc, the firm's chief compliance officer, sitting in one of the chairs opposite Brad's desk.

Gwen slowed to a stop. "Brad." Gwen swallowed, though her mouth was dry. "What's going on?"

Brad closed the door and walked to the other side of his desk. "You know Marc, right?" Brad asked without answering her question.

"I do," Gwen said warily.

"Good. If you wouldn't mind taking a seat." Brad motioned at the other seat across from his desk.

Gwen slid into the seat wordlessly. Her mind kept spinning, trying to come up with why she might be in Brad's office. As far as she knew, she hadn't done anything to warrant this sort of treatment.

"Do you mind if we record this?" Marc asked placidly. If there was any tension in the room, he seemed oblivious to it.

"As I don't know what this is about, yes, I mind." Gwen cut her eyes from Brad to Marc and back to Brad.

"There's been—" Brad started, only to have Marc cut him off.

"Brad—" Marc warned, but Brad held up a hand to stop him.

"There's been an allegation that you're in a sexual relationship with a subordinate." Brad thinned his lips.

Gwen sucked in a breath. She felt like she had been punched in the stomach, but her mind didn't stop working even as she started to feel nauseous. This couldn't be happening. Everything with Etta had been entirely consensual. Etta would have had no reason to tell anyone at the firm about them. Gwen wanted to tell Brad that, but she knew better than to say anything without talking to a lawyer first. This was too serious for her to wing it alone. This could derail everything.

"I won't answer any questions without counsel." She did her best to project a facade of calm while she mentally went through a list of people she could call.

"Of course, but we're going to have to suspend you until the conversation about this happens," Brad replied. For the first time in their long friendship, Brad did not look like her friend. All of his usual charm was gone.

"Fine." Gwen closed her eyes for a moment to let everything sink in, then she opened them again. "Tell Lindsay that my notes about the Singh case are on top of my desk. My car keys are in my purse, which is in my office. Sam can bring them up. I assume someone is going to walk me out?"

"I will." Brad nodded. He picked up his phone and called Sam. The conversation was short, and the room fell into silence. Gwen looked at her watch. It wouldn't take long for Sam to bring her things up. She wondered if they had already talked to Etta, but she didn't ask. She had to assume that they had.

The seconds ticked by on her watch until Brad's door opened and his assistant stepped in carrying Gwen's purse. Gwen took it from her with a quiet, "Thank you," before the woman left the room.

Once she was gone, Brad stood up. Gwen followed him onto her feet, as did Marc. Neither of them said anything as Brad walked her to the elevator. No one would think twice about seeing her with Brad. The same couldn't be said if her escort was a member of security. For that, Gwen was grateful.

The silent elevator ride to the bottom floor seemed to take forever, but Gwen refused to pace. She also knew that trying to make conversation with Brad wouldn't be wise. They transferred from one elevator to the next. That ride was shorter, but just as tense. When they got out, Brad looked like he wanted to say something, but in the end, he kept his silence. Anything either of them said now would be scrutinized later.

Gwen walked over to her car and opened the door. After she sat down, she took another deep breath before she started the car and drove away.

❖

Etta stepped out of the elevator and into the hallway in front of Gwen's condo. Gwen hadn't responded to any of the texts she had sent her that afternoon, but apparently, she was willing to let Etta into the building. She reached for the doorknob. Part of her expected it to be unlocked like it always was, but she knew that it wouldn't be. When it didn't turn in her hand, she tapped on the door.

Gwen opened it almost immediately. She had to have been standing on the other side waiting for Etta to knock.

"You shouldn't be here," Gwen said, preempting Etta, but letting her in all the same.

"But—" Etta tried again. She needed to talk to Gwen, and Gwen wasn't answering her phone. Of course she had gone to her condo. What else was she supposed to do?

"Go home." Gwen held her hands out, palms down.

"You can't expect me to just leave," Etta said. "Look, I don't know who said—"

"It doesn't matter," Gwen said.

"Stop interrupting me. It does matter. I need you to know it wasn't me." Gwen looked haggard in a way that Etta had never seen her, and Etta wanted to soothe her. Gwen wasn't letting her though.

"I didn't think it was. That doesn't change the fact that you shouldn't be here. They're going to ask me if I spoke to you after they suspended me, and now I have to tell them yes. That isn't going to look good." Gwen furrowed her brow and crossed her arms over her chest.

"They suspended you?" Etta's eyes went wide.

"Of course they suspended me. It's sexual harassment lawsuit defense 101." That response made Etta feel young and stupid.

"It wasn't sexual harassment. I don't have any intention of suing them. I told them I wasn't going to sue them," Etta said. Why wasn't anyone listening to her?

"Right now, that doesn't mean anything. And the fact that we're talking only makes everything look worse." Gwen tightened her arms around herself.

"We didn't do anything wrong." Etta wanted to make that clear.

"That doesn't matter. Once I found out that you were going to be working there, nothing should have happened. That should have been the end of it. I should have…" Gwen rubbed her forehead.

"You should have what?" Etta looked at Gwen intently.

"I should have never seen you again." It looked like it pained Gwen to say it, and she couldn't meet Etta's eyes.

"So, what, all of this was a mistake? A lapse in judgment? Something you regret?" Etta needed to know, she needed to know what Gwen was thinking.

"I don't—" Gwen looked away. "If we were going to do this, we should have waited until after the summer was over. Or we should have told someone in HR that we were seeing each other. I should have known better. I should have stopped this."

"You tried, remember? Don't blame yourself for something I did. I'm the one who wanted to keep seeing you. Or is that part not important?" Etta clenched her jaw. This was stupid. Why was everyone acting like she didn't know what she was doing? They hadn't done anything wrong.

"I am sixteen years older than you and a senior partner. No, what you want doesn't matter. No one will care about who instigated what. This was my fault." Gwen finally looked at Etta again. Etta didn't like what she saw in Gwen's eyes.

"This wasn't anyone's fault," she said. Surely, if she said it enough, people would start to believe her. Gwen would start to believe her.

"You are being willfully naive," Gwen replied.

"Fine. Everything was your fault. You seduced me. I never would have slept with you if you hadn't forced yourself on me. Let's completely rewrite history." She knew it was a stupid thing to say, but she couldn't stop herself. She was getting more and more frustrated as this conversation continued. Panic started to well up in her chest. This couldn't be happening.

Gwen put a hand to her forehead. "This isn't productive. You need to leave."

"I'm not going to let some corporate overlord tell me what I can and can't do in my private life," Etta said.

"Etta, you're going to be gone in a month. I'm not. I actually like my job. I'd like to keep it." Gwen replied. Now she sounded irritated.

"So, what? Brad thinks that you're a litigation risk, so we can't see each other anymore?" Etta couldn't believe this. She couldn't believe that Gwen would cave to this.

"No, we can't." Gwen said it matter-of-factly, but she wasn't looking at Etta anymore.

"You don't mean that." Gwen couldn't mean it.

"Etta, you need to go home. You need to focus on finishing your summer. And if I still have a job next week, you need to stay as far away from me as you possibly can. They can't look like they're blaming you. They can't put *any* of this on you. As far as they're concerned, this is all my fault." Now, Gwen sounded patronizing, and Etta couldn't stand that.

"So, I should stay away from you for my own good. Is that it? Or do you need me to stay away so you don't get fired?" Etta asked bitterly.

"It doesn't matter. The end result is the same." Gwen looked completely closed off.

"And what's that end result? It's hard to be in a relationship with someone you can't talk to," Etta said.

Gwen closed her eyes, then opened them again with a determination in them that Etta didn't like. "Our relationship is over."

"Fine. I hope you continue to enjoy your employment at Dunleavy Byrd." Etta barely stopped herself from slamming Gwen's door behind her. One look at the elevator and she knew it would take too long. She headed toward the stairs.

Chapter Eighteen

Etta sat in her car, staring at the passing traffic as her world crumbled around her. It wasn't fair. It wasn't fair that Gwen had ended things at the first sign of trouble. Her cheeks were wet with tears, but she hastily wiped them away. She didn't want to go home. If she went home, she would be reminded of everything she had just lost.

Jorge would let her sleep on his couch, no questions asked, but Jorge was still in Savannah, and she knew she wouldn't make it back to Cartersville that night, let alone all the way to Savannah. Besides, she had work in the morning, assuming she even wanted to go back. Her continued employment was a toss-up.

She only knew one person in Atlanta. Well, she only knew one person she was close enough with to show up on their doorstep at seven o'clock on a Tuesday night. She pulled out her phone to get directions to Grey's house. She had been there before, but she knew how to get there from 95, not Midtown. Once she had a route keyed up, she turned the key in the ignition and put her car in gear. Druid Hills wasn't that far away.

❖

Gwen closed her eyes and leaned back against the door. Etta had left. Everything was over. Whether or not that helped her case remained to be seen. As she stood there, a bone deep weariness overtook her. She looked around her living room and all she could see was Etta. On the couch reading. In the kitchen making drinks. On the balcony, staring out at the view.

Gwen felt like she was suffocating with it. She needed to get out of her condo, but she needed to go somewhere that wouldn't set off any red flags or raise any eyebrows. A bar was out. Really, anywhere that was public was a bad idea.

She had canceled brunch on Grey twice in a row that summer, but their relationship had survived longer absences. She knew, without a doubt, that Grey would be there for her. She sent a text saying she was coming over but leaving out the details of her day. She would tell Grey when she got there.

Grabbing her purse, Gwen looked around her condo once again. Grey's would be better. She could talk to Grey.

❖

Gwen pulled her car into Grey's driveway without bothering to look around. She didn't know many people who lived in Druid Hills, and none of them lived near Grey. She turned her car off and hurried up the stairs. She rang the doorbell, fidgeting as she waited for Grey to answer.

"Now who is it?" she heard Grey say as they opened the door. They sounded mildly exasperated, and Gwen didn't relish the thought of Grey already having company. She didn't want anyone to see her like this. To see her at this moment.

Grey opened the door the rest of the way.

"Gwen?" Grey looked at her in confusion. "What are you doing here?"

"I am having"—Gwen closed her eyes, then opened them again—"an exceptionally terrible day." She could feel the start of tears, but she blinked them away.

Grey held up their hands. "Okay, whoa. I can only deal with so many crises at a time."

Before Grey could elaborate, Gwen saw movement behind them.

"Etta?" The name slipped out of Gwen's mouth unbidden.

"You two know each other?" Grey said as they looked between Etta and Gwen. It only took a second before a lightbulb obviously went off for Grey. "Shit."

Grey pinched the bridge of their nose. "You, stay there." They pointed at Etta, then slipped outside and closed the door behind themself. "Are you a fucking idiot?"

Gwen flinched at Grey's words. She took a sharp breath. "I didn't know she would be here. How was I supposed to know that? I didn't even know you two had met, let alone that she would come to your house."

"That's not what I'm talking about. This should never have become a thing. I warned you about this." Grey gestured emphatically.

"I know you did," Gwen replied, sounding defeated. "Do you think I don't know?"

"You were supposed to be having fun and that was it," Grey said.

"I was having fun, but then things changed, and I don't know, I started to have feelings for her. I didn't want to give her up," Gwen said.

"What? And so now you've broken up with her?" Grey pursed their lips. "Look, we can talk about this later, but you need to not be here right now. This looks terrible."

Gwen closed her eyes again. "I know."

"Go home, Gwen. Or go to Judith's or Lillian's. But you have to go," Grey said.

Gwen nodded and opened her eyes. "All right. You're right. I can't be here. Just, make sure she's okay."

"This is so fucked up." Grey ran their hands through their hair. "I'll call you tomorrow."

Gwen nodded, then she turned back to her car. She didn't know exactly where she was going to go, but she couldn't stay there.

❖

Etta paced in Grey's living room while she waited for them to reappear. She had never in a million years expected Gwen to show up there. She heard the front door close and braced herself for whatever Grey was going to say.

"She's gone." Grey nodded back toward the door.

"How do you guys know each other?" Etta wrapped her arms around herself. Maybe Grey was Gwen's lawyer, but she suspected that wasn't the case.

"Gwen is my best friend. We've known each other since law school." Grey rubbed their forehead as they looked at Etta.

"I should go." Etta immediately headed for the door only for Grey to step in front of her.

"You're not going anywhere. You're too upset, and I won't be responsible for you driving into a tree." They put their hands on Etta's shoulders. "Look, I'll deal with Gwen later. Right now, you need to sit down and tell me what happened. I can't help anyone if I don't know what's going on."

Etta took a shuddering breath. "Yeah, okay." She nodded and headed for Grey's couch.

"Why don't I make us some tea?" Grey asked.

"Sure," Etta replied.

Grey disappeared into the kitchen and Etta looked down at her shoes. What was she doing? What had she been thinking? Gwen wasn't the only one who should have known better. She had practically jumped Gwen at work. It had only been a matter of time until someone found out and said something. She had been so caught up in Gwen that she hadn't been thinking rationally. It shouldn't have happened. Not like it did.

Etta jerked out of her thoughts when Grey reappeared, two steaming mugs in their hands. They put them both down on the coffee table.

"So, you're Gwen's law student." Grey sat down and leaned against the arm of the couch.

Etta bristled. "I don't belong to anyone."

"Funny, she said that too." Grey scratched the top of their head.

"I'm sure I'll get Gwen's version tomorrow, but why don't you tell me what happened to you?"

Etta took a deep breath. "My section head showed up at my cubicle this morning and told me that the managing director wanted to see me and that I should go up to his office ASAP. I didn't know why I was going up there. I had never even met the managing director before. I mean, Gwen had mentioned him a few times, and it seemed like they were friends, but that didn't have anything to do with me."

Etta looked down at her hands. "I got up there and his assistant let me straight back. There was this guy from compliance, I don't remember his name, he was there too." Etta picked up her tea, but it was still too hot. She put it back down.

"They said there had been a report that I was having an intimate relationship with a senior partner. I couldn't exactly deny it. I asked them what the problem was, and they went into this whole, long thing about how I shouldn't be afraid to say something if I felt like I was being taken advantage of, that there were resources at the firm for people in situations like mine. They made everything seem corrupt and wrong."

Etta squirmed. "I didn't know what to do, but I knew that Gwen hadn't coerced me. I told them that much. I said that everything had been voluntary on my part and that Gwen and I knew each other before I even started working there. I'm not sure I should have said that. I don't know. I just know that Gwen didn't do anything wrong, and I didn't do anything wrong, and they can go fuck themselves for implying otherwise." She picked up her tea again, took a sip without thinking, and burned her tongue.

"I tried to go talk to Gwen about it, but she kept saying I shouldn't be there. Then she broke up with me. I didn't want to be alone, and I didn't know where else to go, so I came here. I didn't know you were friends." Etta closed her eyes. She opened them again when she felt Grey put their hand on her knee.

"Hey, it's going to be okay. Assuming what you said is true"—Grey held up a hand to forestall Etta's objections—"and I don't have any reason to believe that it isn't, everything will be fine. No one is going to come after you. It would look bad. And without a complaint, they can't do much to Gwen. She'll get a slap on the wrist for not telling HR. They'll probably put something in her employment file and be done with it."

"That doesn't change the fact that she said she cared more about her job than me, or the fact that as soon as something bad happened, she broke up with me," Etta pointed out. That was the problem. Etta cared much more about that than she did the investigation.

"Yeah, I know." Grey inhaled then exhaled quickly. "I don't know if I can say anything that'll make that better. The only thing I can tell you to do is drink your tea, go to bed, and see how you feel in the morning. Things will look different if you give them some space."

Etta nodded. "I think I'll do that. Can I stay here?" She felt so tired now.

"Of course. Same room as always." Grey motioned with their head to the hallway where all of the bedrooms were located.

"Thanks." Etta stood up and picked up her tea. "I'm going to go to bed now."

"All right." Grey looked up at her. Etta could tell that they were still concerned. "If you need anything in the night, you know where I'll be."

Etta nodded and said, "Thanks," again before turning down the hallway and finding her bedroom.

❖

Gwen looked up at Judith's house and swallowed. She didn't want to go in, but she didn't want to go home either. She knew this wasn't something that her big sister could get her out of. Still, after telling her she had been an idiot, Judith would still take her side.

Gwen forced herself out of her car and up the walkway to Judith's imposing home. She stepped up to the door and knocked. There wasn't an immediate answer. Gwen was ready to go back to her car when the door opened.

"Gwen?" Judith asked as she took in Gwen's sudden appearance on her doorstep. "Is everything all right?"

Gwen opened her mouth to answer, but nothing came out. Instead, she threw herself forward into Judith's arms. Without asking any more questions, Judith hugged her back.

"Whatever it is, we'll figure it out, okay?" Judith rubbed a hand down Gwen's back. "Come inside. Everything's going to be okay."

Gwen nodded against her sister's neck and stepped back far enough to be able to walk inside.

CHAPTER NINETEEN

Gwen was startled when her phone rang. A glance at the screen showed her the doorman's number. She answered the call hoping Etta wasn't trying to see her again. She didn't know if she could handle another confrontation.

She answered the phone and was relieved to know that Grey was standing in the lobby and not Etta. She instructed the doorman to let them up and then walked over to her front door to open it. While she waited for Grey to join her, she went to the kitchen and poured them both glasses of iced tea. She was tempted to reach for something stronger, but this wasn't the time to take up day drinking. She had just finished setting the glasses out when Grey pushed open her door.

"So," Grey said as they closed the door behind themself.

"Yeah." Gwen took a slow breath. She closed her eyes and rubbed a hand across her forehead.

"What were you thinking?" Grey said as they walked the rest of the way into the condo.

"I wasn't." Gwen shrugged helplessly. "I just…I wasn't. It was immeasurably stupid of me."

Grey reached for their glass of tea and took a sip. "You've hired someone?"

"I have. He's negotiating a time for me to come in and answer questions." Gwen spread her hands against the counter, then balled them into fists. She looked out the window and stared at the skyline for a moment before turning her attention back to Grey. "How's Etta?"

Grey looked at Gwen sympathetically. "She went to work this morning. Beyond that, you'll have to ask her."

"Thank you for being there for her," Gwen said.

"I don't need your thanks. She's a friend. I would have been there for her either way," Grey replied.

"Still." Gwen picked up her tea but didn't take a sip before she put it down again.

"Are you in love with her?" Grey asked. They looked at Gwen intently.

Gwen looked away. "It doesn't matter now. I doubt I'll be allowed to see her between now and the end of the summer. She'll have moved on by then."

"You can't know that." Grey reached for Gwen's hand and squeezed it.

"Yes, I can. Everyone moves on eventually. Better to let her go now than prolong the inevitable." Gwen extracted her hand from Grey's and wrapped it around her tea. This time, she did take a sip.

"You're being fatalistic," Grey said.

"I'm being realistic," Gwen replied. Her phone started to ring, and she flipped it over to see who was calling. "It's my lawyer. I have to take this." She swiped to answer the call, then lifted the phone to her ear.

Grey reached for Gwen's hand again and squeezed it, then they whispered, "Call me if you need anything," and got a nod in return before leaving Gwen's condo.

❖

"Thank you for coming in," Brad said as Gwen stepped into the conference room. She wanted to snap back, but she restrained herself.

"Thank you for having me," Gwen replied. Her lawyer followed her into the room, and everyone made a round of unnecessary introductions. They all already knew each other, but the situation demanded certain pleasantries.

"Shall we get down to it?" Brad asked the room.

"We're ready." James, Gwen's lawyer, responded for both of them. Marc started the voice recorder.

"Gwen, I know you already know this, but as this is an internal matter, we're going to require you to answer our questions fully and truthfully. If you don't, we can take disciplinary actions up to and including termination." Brad looked searchingly at Gwen, as if he could will her to tell the truth.

"I understand." Gwen felt nauseous. She wasn't afraid of their questions. Beyond failing to inform HR that she was dating someone at the firm, she hadn't done anything wrong. She hadn't forced Etta to do anything, nor had she pulled any strings for Etta once she knew Etta was working at the firm.

"Good. Marc is going to be the one asking the questions, so I'll turn this over to him." Brad looked at Marc and nodded.

"Thank you," Marc said. "Ms. Strickland, we have several questions for you. We would like to start with when you first met Ms. Monroe and the circumstances surrounding that meeting."

"I understand." It was a scripted question, but Gwen was glad to have a script to follow. She knew the rest of the questions would be much harder to answer. She took a quick moment to center herself. She could do this.

❖

Gwen unlocked the door to her condo and slowly walked inside. She was exhausted. She grabbed her phone, tossed her bag down by the door, then collapsed on the couch. It was over. She had answered all of their questions and now she didn't have to worry about it anymore.

She opened her phone and tapped Grey's number.

Grey picked up on the first ring.

"What happened?" Grey asked immediately.

"An unpaid suspension for the next two and a half weeks, until the summer program is over. A confidential letter of reprimand in my employee file. They don't want me to see her again, but can't mandate it. That shouldn't be a problem, though. I doubt she wants to see me." She didn't bother rehashing what had happened at the hearing. That was the information Grey wanted.

"That's a lot better than it could have been." Grey sounded relieved. Gwen just felt tired.

"Yeah, I've still got a job at least." Gwen closed her eyes and let her head drop back onto the top of the couch.

"That's what you wanted out of this, right?" If there was judgment in Grey's tone, Gwen didn't hear it.

"Right. Look, I need to call Judith. I'll talk to you later, okay?" Gwen wanted to go to bed and never get out of it. She guessed she had two and a half weeks to do just that. But first, Judith would want to know what happened too.

"Okay, but we are having brunch this Saturday. I'm not hearing any excuses about how you're too busy." Grey was using the tone that said they would come to Gwen's condo and drag her out of bed if necessary.

"All right." It was easier to agree than anything else. They said their goodbyes and Gwen scrolled through her phone to Judith's number. She would make this call and then she would allow herself to crash.

Chapter Twenty

Etta pulled her car into the parking lot attached to Jorge and Dom's apartment building in Savannah. She thought she was near his apartment, but all of the buildings looked the same and the numbers were hard to read. She pulled out her phone and called him.

Jorge didn't answer right away, but she saw him standing in a now open doorway, the light from his apartment outlining him. She hung up and got out of her car. It took a second to grab her bag from the back seat of her car, and by then he was headed in her direction.

They met up on the sidewalk and Etta threw herself into his open arms. He had always given the best hugs, and this time was no exception.

"So, you texted me that you were coming to crash on my couch for the weekend, but you refused to answer my follow-up texts. You're always welcome to hang, but what's going on?" Jorge finally let Etta go.

"Oh, buddy." Etta felt exhausted, but she needed to explain things to Jorge. "I have not been good enough at keeping in touch. The short version?"

"Yeah, sure." Jorge looked at her in curiosity.

"Shit's fucked, man." Etta looked up at him. She was so glad to see him again. When she added that to not being in Atlanta for the weekend, she almost managed a good mood.

"Okay, come inside and give me and Dom the slightly longer version." Jorge took her bag from her, then draped his free arm over her shoulder.

The walk up to his second-floor apartment only took a few minutes. Before she knew it, Etta was standing in Jorge and Dom's living room. Dom gave her a more sedate hug, but Etta welcomed it too.

"Do you want something to drink?" Jorge asked as he put her bag down near the couch.

"That depends entirely on how much tequila you have." Etta meant it as a joke, but it missed the mark and came out as a sincere request.

Jorge looked at her more intently. "Shit really is fucked, isn't it?"

"Yeah. Yeah, it really is." Etta sat on the couch and grabbed one of the throw pillows to wrap her arms around.

"Then I'll get the tequila. We should have some orange juice we can mix it with or something. You're not allowed to do shots of it before you tell us the whole story." Jorge disappeared into the kitchen as Dom pulled a rolling desk chair into the living room. There weren't a lot of other seating options.

"How's your summer been?" Etta asked her to make small talk. She liked Dom, but she didn't know her as well as she knew Jorge. She felt awkward sitting in a room alone with her.

"It's been good. Hectic, but good. I've even managed to help a few people." Dom smiled. Before she could ask a reciprocal question, Jorge reappeared with a bottle of tequila, a carton of orange juice, and three glasses of ice. He looked like he was about to drop something, but he managed to make it to the dining room table before anything crashed out of his hands.

"That's great." Etta nodded as she watched Jorge pour a healthy amount of tequila into a glass and then splash orange juice into it. He did it three times before he handed the glasses to Etta and Dom.

Etta took a sip and nearly coughed at how much tequila was in the glass. It was a very good thing that working at the Bear's Den only involved wine and beer. No one would ever mistake Jorge for a real bartender.

"Now that you've been properly lubricated, what's going on?" Jorge prodded as he sat on the couch near Etta.

Etta took another sip. The drink was growing on her. "You remember the lawyer from the bar? The one I hooked up with?"

"The hot MILF?" Jorge replied only to have Dom slap the back of his head. "Sorry! Sorry. But yeah. Hot, blond, arrogant as all fuck?"

"That's her." Etta smiled at the memory of Gwen standing at the bar drinking martinis and insulting everyone else in the bar as she did so.

"The last I heard, you were going to have dinner at her place. But that was back in April, right before classes got out for the semester." Jorge scratched at his beard.

"Yeah. Turns out we work at the same place, and I might have kept seeing her." Etta took a bigger sip of her drink.

"Okay, but what's the problem? Last I checked, you're allowed to date whoever you want to date." Jorge looked at her in confusion.

"You fell in love with her and then the firm found out." Dom finished the story for Etta.

"Right in one." Etta put her drink down and ran a hand through her hair.

"She broke up with you?" Dom asked, though Etta wondered if it was really a question or just a confirmation of suspicions.

"Also correct." Etta rubbed her forehead. "My house in Atlanta reminds me of her, and I couldn't stay there this weekend. Thank you for letting me spend the weekend here instead."

"Do you have to see her at work?" Dom looked at her in concern.

"No." Etta picked her drink back up. She wanted the oblivion the tequila would grant her. "She's been suspended until after I leave. At least, that's what they told me. She hasn't spoken to me since the day everything imploded."

Dom looked at Etta with sympathy. She grabbed the bottle of tequila and unscrewed the top, then held it out to Etta. "Go ahead and get wasted. You'll feel terrible tomorrow, but maybe it'll help."

Etta smiled weakly. "Thanks." She took the bottle from Dom and poured more of it into her orange juice. It was nearly undrinkable when she tasted it, but she swallowed it anyway. The faster she drank, the faster she wouldn't be able to feel it anymore. She knew it wasn't healthy, but it was the weekend. She didn't have any responsibilities until Sunday night when she drove back to Atlanta. She could afford to spend some time in the bottom of a bottle.

❖

Etta took a deep breath of sea air, then rolled from her stomach to her back. She had been spectacularly hung over when she had woken up that morning, but it was midafternoon now, and her head had finally cleared. She pushed her toes into the sand, scrunching them up and then relaxing them. Tybee Island had the closest beach to Savannah, and that was good enough for Etta.

"What are you thinking about?" Jorge asked. He was sitting on a towel next to hers with Dom on his other side. Dom's black skin gleamed in the sun, and Jorge was turning a darker brown. Etta felt pale next to them.

"That we're a long way from Antigua," Etta said.

"That's true. Why are you thinking about Antigua, of all places?" Jorge looked down at her.

"Gwen wanted to take me there in early August." Etta held her hands up and looked at them. Maybe she was getting something that resembled a tan after all. "I told her she wasn't allowed to plan a vacation that involved leaving the United States."

"She wanted to take you on a Caribbean vacation, and you said no?" Dom sounded incredulous.

Etta shrugged. "It seemed excessive. Maybe if it had been next summer…" She swallowed down the emotions that she didn't want to overwhelm her. "There's no point thinking about it. There won't be any trips now."

Jorge squeezed her shoulder with a slightly sandy hand. "You'll find someone else to go on tropical vacations with."

"Yeah." Etta looked out at the ocean. "The problem is, right now I don't want to go on vacation with anyone else."

"That'll pass," Dom said gently. "I promise you, you'll get over her. It might take some time, but you will."

"Thanks." Etta wiped her palms on her towel before swinging her legs to the side and standing up. "I'm going to go get in the water. Either of you coming?"

"Yeah, I'll come with you." Jorge pushed himself into a standing position next to her. "Wanna race?"

"Your legs are, like, six feet longer than mine," Etta replied as she started walking toward the water.

Jorge smiled. He said, "You're no fun," as he started walking beside her.

❖

"You know you can come back next weekend, if you want," Jorge said as he leaned into her passenger side window. Etta was getting ready to drive back to Atlanta. She didn't particularly want to go back, but she had work the next morning.

"I know. The firm is taking us to a Braves game, though. They got a box and everything." Baseball wasn't her thing, but she guessed the firm had needed to do something since Gwen's dinner party had been canceled at the last minute. The firm hadn't given a reason, though it was no mystery to Etta. She was certain that there were rumors flying about it, but no one had said anything to her face yet, and she appreciated that.

"Sweet." Jorge extricated himself from her window and took a step back. "But if you change your mind, we'll be here."

"Thanks." Etta tried to put on a good face, but she suspected it wasn't entirely convincing.

"Have a good drive. Text me when you get there," Jorge added.

"I will." Etta rolled up her window and put her car into reverse. She would get back to Atlanta around ten. At least, that was the plan. After that, well, it would be time to go to bed, leaving her no time to think about all of the things she didn't want to think about.

Chapter Twenty-one

G wen sat restlessly at the table, bouncing her knee in agitation. Grey had stepped away to the restroom. It was the second week in a row that Grey had insisted they have brunch together. The second weekend of her exile from the firm. She knew no one in the restaurant was paying attention to her, but she felt eyes on her nevertheless.

"Gwen," a man's voice nearly boomed from beside her and she jumped out of her skin. After catching her breath, Gwen looked up to see who it was. Judge Wilcox held a hand out for her to shake. They only knew each other in passing, but he was a member of the nominating commission.

She took his hand and shook it. "Judge Wilcox, what can I do for you?"

"I wanted to come over and say that I saw your name on the list of interested parties for the supreme court vacancy. I hope your application is as impressive as I assume it will be." He looked downright jolly, which didn't fit Gwen's mood at all. He leaned closer as he let go of her hand. "But you should know that there's a nasty rumor going around right now. You'll need to make sure you've cleaned that up before the interviews start."

"Thank you for letting me know." Gwen appreciated the heads-up, but she didn't know what she could do about any rumors that were swirling about her in the legal community. Particularly as they likely contained some bit of truth.

"Well, I just wanted to come say hello." He patted her on the shoulder. "Good luck with everything."

"Thank you." Gwen couldn't say anything else. The judge didn't seem to think there was anything amiss about that as he wove his way through the tables toward the door. She watched him go.

Grey appeared a moment later. "What did Judge Wilcox want?" they asked as they sat down.

"To warn me about some rumors and wish me luck on my supreme court application." Gwen watched him walk away and then refocused on Grey. "I'm thinking about rescinding it."

"Your application? Why would you do that?" Grey asked as the two of them waited for the server to come take their order.

"You know why." Gwen gave Grey a significant look. There was no point in Grey pretending to be obtuse.

"Don't do anything hasty. They're just rumors. No one who actually knows anything is going to be talking. All the rest have are suppositions." Grey reached out for Gwen's hand and squeezed it.

"And if their suppositions are worse than reality? You know how these things go. I'm sure the rumors are painting me in a much worse light than the truth would." Gwen squeezed Grey's hand back.

"Then you'll go into the interview and tell the truth. Tell them that you regret the actions that got you to the place where people doubt your integrity. Tell them that the relationship is over. Tell them that you learned a valuable lesson that you'll carry forward into the future, and that you would never do anything to besmirch the dignity of the court. You made a bad decision. It wasn't like they caught you trying to bribe someone, or lying," Grey said, and Gwen was willing to admit it was a good plan. Or at least the best plan she had.

"That assumes I even get an interview," Gwen replied. There was every chance that the rumors would scuttle everything.

"You'll get an interview. You're too qualified to not get one," Grey said. "This won't destroy your future."

"I hope you're right," Gwen replied, before she glanced down at the menu. She already knew what she wanted, but she needed to escape Grey's scrutiny for a moment.

"I know I am." Grey leaned back in their chair and crossed their legs. "Besides, when have I ever been wrong?"

"All the time, Grey. All the time," Gwen retorted as the server finally approached their table.

❖

Etta leaned back in her seat and looked out over the baseball diamond that stretched out in front of her. These were, without a doubt, the nicest seats at a baseball game she had ever experienced. She didn't follow the sport, but she knew enough to know what was going on down on the field. The Braves were playing the Nationals, but Etta didn't know who was ahead in the standings, or even the series. That night, the Braves were up 3–2, and the baseball aficionados in the group kept muttering about defense. For the most part, she tuned them out.

"You don't look like you're having a good time." A voice interrupted her thoughts and she turned toward it. Brad was standing in the aisle next to her row of seats, a drink in his hand.

"I'm fine." Etta looked up at him. Of all the people she wanted to talk to, Brad was at the bottom of her list.

"So, what's your sport?" Brad sat down, an empty seat between them.

"Women's college basketball." No matter how much she didn't want to talk to Brad, she was going to be polite. He was her boss for another week. She needed to act like it. If that meant small talk, then that's what she would do. "Stanford," she supplied before he could ask.

"That's where you went to undergrad?" he asked.

"Yeah." Etta nodded. She wanted out of this conversation. "But I'm from Columbus. Georgia, not Ohio. I wanted to be closer to family, and T.R. is the best law school in the South."

"And you want to stay in Atlanta?" Brad took a sip of his drink. Both of their attentions were dragged away from the conversation by the crack of a bat and then a raucous cheer: 4–2.

Gwen turned back to Brad. "Yes. I want to stay in Atlanta."

"Then I'm hoping the recent unpleasantness won't interfere with your acceptance of the job we'd like to offer you." Brad looked at her expectantly.

"Mr. Whitaker, don't take this the wrong way, but I have no desire to work for you. I realized pretty quickly that I don't want to spend my life working for soulless corporations. That was before you destroyed the only good thing about this summer. So yes, it is about the *recent unpleasantness*. I know you were just doing your job, but you didn't do me any favors. Believe what you want, but my relationship with Gwen was real, and now she won't even talk to me." Etta glared at him. In that moment, she didn't care about how much sway he might have over her future career. She needed him to hear her. Gwen might not listen to her, but *Brad* would have to.

"I'm not going to live in a world where the woman I love is three floors away and I can't see her because of your rules. She didn't take advantage of me. We didn't do anything wrong. And I resent the fact that you seem to want me to feel like we did. I know that you and Gwen are friends, or you were, but I really hope she gets that supreme court appointment and you have to learn to live without her too." Etta stood up and slid by Brad into the aisle.

"Enjoy the rest of the game. I'm going to go home. Baseball really isn't my sport." Etta didn't wait for a response. She turned away from Brad and climbed the stairs into the box. Her heart still ached, and she still had tears left to cry over the implosion of her relationship with Gwen, but a small part of her felt better, felt vindicated. At least one person knew how she felt and had to respect her choices. Without bothering to say good-bye to anyone, she walked out of the box and headed home.

❖

Gwen sipped her wine as she stared out over the Atlanta skyline. Judith and Lillian were waiting for her to bring the bottle back over to the couches with her, but she was having a hard time focusing.

She startled when she felt a hand on the back of her arm.

"I'll take this," Lillian said as she liberated the bottle from

Gwen's hold. "Come sit back down. Moping on the couch is more comfortable than moping over here."

"I'm not moping," Gwen replied petulantly, but she did as Lillian directed.

"You are." Judith's voice reached across the room.

Gwen rubbed her eyes as she retook her seat on the couch. "What do I get if I admit that I'm moping?"

"Nothing. Now, is it the job, the supreme court thing, or the girl?" Judith asked.

"She's not a girl," Gwen replied. She almost regretted telling Judith everything the night she had gone to visit. Judith had been there for her, though, so she couldn't regret it too much.

"So, it's the girl, then," Judith said, as if she knew the secrets of the universe, or at least the universe of Gwen.

Gwen closed her eyes. "Do we have to do this?"

"Yes," Lillian said.

Gwen rubbed her forehead. "I need to get over it. I..." She sighed heavily. "I need to stop thinking about her."

"Easier said than done," Lillian said. "I tried to forget about Leo for months after he got me pregnant. It never worked."

"And you've been happily married for almost two decades. Yes, I know. This isn't the same thing." Gwen was happy that things had worked out so well for Lillian, but her life didn't work that way.

"Why isn't it? You're in love with her, aren't you?" Judith never was one for sugarcoating things.

"I'm sixteen years older than her. I can't..." Gwen looked at Judith helplessly. They didn't understand. It wouldn't work out. It was never going to work out. She had been delusional to think that it would.

"Did she know you were sixteen years older than her?" Judith insisted.

"Yes, but—"

"Did she care?" Judith was worse than a prosecutor when it came to getting answers to her questions in order to make a point.

"She didn't seem to." Gwen couldn't think of a time when Etta had even hinted that Gwen's age bothered her.

"Then why do you?" Judith looked at Gwen intently. "You didn't force her to be in a relationship with you. You didn't make her sleep with you. She's responsible for what she did too. Get over yourself."

"Are you finished?" Gwen was ready for this visit to end. She didn't need Judith to point out everything she had done wrong over the past three weeks.

"Do you need me to keep going?" Judith replied, looking determined.

"No. I don't." Gwen pursed her lips. It didn't matter that what Judith said made sense. She wasn't ready to hear it.

"Good. Now, how's the supreme court thing going?" Judith's change of subject didn't make Gwen any happier.

"I have an interview with a subcommittee the Tuesday after next," Gwen said. She still didn't know how she was going to address whatever rumors were spinning around about her.

"They're moving fast," Lillian replied.

"Yeah. The August term is about to start. They probably won't have anyone appointed by then, but they won't want things to drag on either." Gwen let her head fall back on to the top of the couch.

"What are you going to say at your interview?" Judith asked. "You'll have to address everything, won't you?"

"Grey has a strategy." Gwen lifted her head back up. "With as much time as they spend trying to convince politicians to do what they want, they're actually pretty good at this sort of thing."

"Then you'll do what Grey tells you to, and by Christmas we'll be having dinner with a supreme court justice." Judith smiled, ruthlessness tugging at her lips.

"You're going to jinx it." Gwen took a sip of her wine.

Judith waved her off and turned the subject to Lillian's children.

❖

"Hey, Mom," Etta said as her mom answered the phone. Part of her had been hoping to be able to leave a voicemail, but she knew she'd have to talk to her mom eventually. The sooner she got this over with, well, the sooner her mom would stop pestering her about it. There wouldn't be any getting out of that.

"Etta, it's so good to hear from you. I feel like it's been forever since we talked."

Etta closed her eyes. She really wasn't in the mood for her mother's passive-aggressive attempts to guilt her. "It's only been a few weeks."

"A month. It's been a month," her mom pointed out. Etta tried not to sigh. "Your summer thing is almost over, isn't it? Have they offered you a job? I hear that's how those things are supposed to go."

Etta took a deep breath and released it slowly. Time to jump into the deep end. "Yes, they offered me a job—"

"That's fantastic! When do you start? After the bar, obviously—" Etta's mother spun off into her own world.

"I didn't accept it." Etta braced herself for the coming reaction.

"I'm sorry, I must have misheard you. Did you say you didn't take it?" Her mom sounded incredulous.

"Yeah. I didn't take it. It's not the kind of law I want to practice. I pretty much hated the work. I'll be miserable if I work there." Etta knew that her mom wouldn't accept her reasoning, but she had to put it out there.

"Well, that's just ridiculous. You had a guaranteed job for after graduation and you turned it down? Do you know how many people would kill to be in your position? Why would you throw away your future like that?"

"I'm not throwing my future away. I'll get a job. It just won't be doing that." Etta tried to keep it together. She'd known her mom wouldn't be happy when she found out Etta's plans, but she wasn't prepared to lie about them. Still, it hurt that her mom couldn't support what she wanted.

"I can't talk to you when you're like this," her mom said. "Call me back when you've come to your senses."

Etta looked at the phone. Her mom had hung up on her. She promised herself she wasn't going to cry. She had already cried more in July than she had the entire rest of the year. Still, it stung.

Chapter Twenty-two

I am absolutely positive that I don't need your help. If you drive up here to move two suitcases and two boxes, I will not provide pizza or beer when we get back to Cartersville. You've got another week in Savannah. Do not spend your last weekend there doing this. Go to the beach. Take Dom somewhere fancy for dinner on River Street. Do not drive all the way to Atlanta to help me do something I can do myself in fifteen minutes." Etta tried to communicate her seriousness to Jorge as emphatically as she could.

"All right. Fine. I won't drive to Atlanta. But you'll let me know when you get back to Cartersville, right?" Jorge asked.

Etta really was thankful to have a friend as loyal as Jorge, but sometimes he could get a tad overbearing. Still, it was nice to know that someone cared about her. Someone who wouldn't disappear at the first sign of trouble.

Etta closed her eyes and tried to push away her thoughts about Gwen. They didn't do any good. Gwen wasn't coming back.

"Yeah. I'll let you know when I get home," Etta replied.

"Good," Jorge said. "Hey, didn't you only have one box when you moved up there?"

"I collected a few things. No, it isn't all books." Etta preempted his question. He knew her too well sometimes. "Now, let me get back to my packing."

"Okay. You know if you need anything, you just have to call, right?" Jorge prodded.

"I know. And I'm hanging up now," Etta said.

"Okay. Have a good drive tomorrow," Jorge replied.

"I will. And I'll talk to you later." With that, Etta hung up the phone. She looked around the house for anything that she might have missed, but she didn't see anything. She moved into the bedroom to finish packing her suitcase. Most of her clothes were already in there, but she still had a drawer to go. She opened it and had to stop. It was mostly full of loungewear, and right on the top were a pair of Gwen's yoga pants and the T-shirt Etta had loaned her after they had spent their first night together.

The T-shirt hadn't meant anything when Etta had loaned it to Gwen, but now it felt both like a punch to the gut and a lifeline. She picked it up and held it to her face, hoping it had retained some hint of Gwen's perfume. Instead, it smelled like her own laundry detergent.

Etta rubbed the back of her neck and scoffed at her own flight of fancy before she tossed the clothing toward her suitcase. She would need to return the pants eventually, but she doubted Gwen would let her up to her condo. She'd ship them back once she got to Cartersville.

With the last drawer emptied, Etta zipped up her suitcase. The only things still out were her pajamas and her clothes for the next day. Her current clothing and her pajamas would be easy enough to stuff into a side pocket in the morning.

She would take the boxes and one of the suitcases out to her car tonight and pick up the last one in the morning. By this time tomorrow, she would be back in her own apartment, getting ready to get into her own bed. Maybe then she wouldn't be surrounded by things that reminded her of Gwen, and she could start to get over her.

❖

Gwen stretched her legs out and rubbed her eyes. It had been a long afternoon. There were cartons of cold Chinese littering the tabletop where they had been sitting in Grey's office. She was ready for the practice session to end, but the day wasn't over yet. "Do you think we might wrap this up sometime soon?" she asked Grey.

"Do you want this seat?" Grey looked at Gwen pointedly.

"Yes. Of course," Gwen replied, though she was starting to have some reservations. Not about the position itself, but about what it seemed like she would need to say to get it.

She and Grey had already been over the standard questions that they thought the interview committee would ask. Now they were on to the ones Gwen would have a harder time answering.

"But we've been doing this all day. I'm tired and I think we're going around in circles." Gwen tucked her feet back under the chair and sat up straight again.

"Give me another half an hour and then we'll stop," Grey said. They crossed their arms and looked at Gwen sternly.

"Fine. Let's go over it one more time." Gwen blinked and tried to clear her head. Her eyes were bleary, but rubbing them hadn't helped before, so she didn't bother.

"Okay. So, you're sitting with the interview committee. You've already answered all of their substantive questions. It's the end of the interview and you're tired. Then they come at you with something like, 'There's been a rumor that you were having an inappropriate sexual relationship with a subordinate. Is that true?'"

Gwen closed her eyes for a minute thinking about everything she and Grey had talked about. Keep it simple. Stick to the truth. Don't embellish anything.

"Yes. Although she wasn't my subordinate when the relationship began."

They had started their strategy session assuming Gwen would be given time to follow up on her answers. This wasn't supposed to be a cross-examination, after all.

"So, what was she?" Grey followed up.

"A law student," Gwen replied. She hoped that they wouldn't ask that question, but she couldn't count on it.

"And you didn't think that was inappropriate?" Grey pushed.

"She is a twenty-eight-year-old adult. Last I checked, that's far past the age of consent."

"Don't get defensive," Grey said.

"Right." Gwen took a breath. "Right." She futilely rubbed her eyes. It was getting late, and her nerves were starting to fray. "The relationship was a lapse in judgment. It isn't a mistake I'll make again."

"If you've had one lapse in judgment, why should we believe that you won't have another one? One that involves the law rather than simply a personal matter?" Grey went back to playing the interviewer.

"I think my professional record speaks for itself. I've worked hard throughout my career to make sure I was interpreting the law to the best of my ability and in my clients' best interest. As you can see from the rest of my application, my legal work is impeccable," Gwen replied.

"Good." Grey nodded. "I think you're as ready as you can get." They checked their watch. "And it only took fifteen minutes instead of thirty."

"So, we're finished?" Gwen slumped back in her chair.

"We're finished." Grey stood up and walked the few feet over to Gwen. They put a hand on Gwen's shoulder and squeezed it. "You're going to knock this out of the park."

Gwen wrapped her hand around Grey's wrist, rubbing her thumb against it. She looked up at them. "Thank you."

"Not necessary," Grey said. They waved off the sentiment, then stepped away. "Now, go home, take a bath or something, just chill for the rest of the day, and get some sleep tonight. You can do this. Do I need to show up tomorrow morning and give you another pep talk?"

Gwen laughed. "I'll be fine. No early morning pep talk necessary."

"Okay. I'll stay home. But I'll be rooting for you," Grey said.

"And I'll call you as soon as it's over," Gwen offered.

"You'd better." Grey started cleaning up the Chinese. "Now, let's get out of here."

"All right." Gwen heaved herself up. As soon as Grey finished cleaning up, the two of them walked out of the office. Gwen got into her car and headed home.

❖

Etta pulled into the gravel lot by her apartment and threw her car into park. She'd ended up leaving Atlanta far later than she had planned, and it was late afternoon before she made it back to Cartersville. Moving was always tiring, even though she hadn't had much to move. She wasn't looking forward to dragging everything upstairs. She was tempted to leave all of it in the car until the next day. She didn't have any plans for her Monday yet. She could worry about it later.

Getting out of her car, Etta looked toward the door to her apartment, only to sigh in exasperation. There were benches on either side of the walkway leading up to her door. Sometimes, a delivery person would leave packages on them. Today, someone had left Jorge. His bulk was impossible to hide behind the plant life.

"You're not supposed to be here." Etta gave him an unamused look. "In fact, you promised me that you wouldn't be here."

"Ah, see that's where you're wrong." Jorge held up a finger. "I promised you that I wouldn't drive to Atlanta. I didn't say anything about Cartersville."

"Semantics," Etta said as she narrowed her eyes. She wasn't actually all that upset, but it wouldn't do to let Jorge know that.

"We're lawyers, Etta. Words have meaning." Jorge wagged a finger.

"Stop quoting Professor Brightman at me." Etta pulled out her keys and unlocked the door at the bottom of the stairs.

"Professor Brightman is a very smart woman." Jorge grabbed the door and held it open for Etta before following her inside and up the stairs. Etta let them both into her apartment and she flicked the lights on. There was a bit of dust on everything, but she could take care of that sometime over the next week. Her beach trip with Gwen wasn't happening, so she wasn't doing anything else that week. "So, should I go get your stuff out of your car?"

"Yes." She used her hands to shoo him in the direction of the door. "But you get to carry all of it since you came here against my wishes."

"It's two suitcases and two boxes, right?" Jorge looked at her for confirmation.

"Yeah. The car's still unlocked," Etta replied.

"Cool. I'll be right back." Jorge bounded out of the apartment and down the stairs. Sometimes, Etta forgot that he was only twenty-three, but in that moment, she felt every year between them. She didn't have that sort of energy after an hour-and-a-half-long drive. She wondered if Gwen had ever felt the age difference between them in that way—as if Etta was painfully younger than her. If she had, she hadn't said anything.

A minute later, Jorge stepped back into the apartment with a suitcase in each hand. He set them down gently and turned to go down the stairs again. Etta thought about helping him. It really wasn't nice of her to make him lift all of the heavy things, but then again, she had told him not to visit in the first place. She left him to the boxes.

❖

Gwen couldn't sleep. She rarely had problems sleeping. It didn't matter how important the court case was, she could sleep the night before the hearing. She'd slept before her very first trial. She'd slept before her very first supreme court oral argument. She'd slept before the last one.

Tonight, she couldn't sleep. She'd tossed. She'd turned. She'd counted sheep. She'd tried a white noise app on her phone. She'd scrounged up some lavender linen spray that Lillian had gotten her as a gift at some fuzzy point in the past. The only thing she hadn't tried were sleeping pills. She couldn't afford to feel drugged and drowsy the next day.

She knew looking at her phone was detrimental to her attempts to sleep, but she picked it up anyway. Two thirty-eight a.m. She checked her email, but there was nothing new. Neither were there any new messages from Grey or her sisters.

It was masochistic, but she looked at her text chain with Etta. She scrolled up as far as she could in a few seconds and then started reading the texts in order. She loved the way that Etta flirted with her over text. Her dry wit and her deadpan replies to the things Gwen said still made her laugh, but now that laughter was full of regret and sadness. Despite her practiced answer, she didn't regret her relationship with Etta. It had been the highlight of her summer. It once had the possibility of being much more than that. No, Gwen regretted the way things had ended, but she didn't regret the relationship at all.

Gwen got to the texts that she hadn't answered the day of the investigation, and she stopped reading, scrolling to the bottom of the messages. She wanted to text Etta, though she didn't know what she would say. It would have to start with an apology, but after that, all she wanted was to see Etta again. She wanted Etta by her side in bed that night. She wanted Etta to be waiting for her after her interview. She wanted Etta with her no matter what the outcome might be. She just wanted Etta.

Gwen put down the phone before she could do something imprudent, and she rolled back over. Grey would be so proud of her.

Chapter Twenty-three

Gwen glanced up toward the sun as she left the Dunleavy Byrd offices. It was swelteringly hot out, and Gwen immediately regretted that she had to wear a suit to her interview. They were conducting it at a firm down the street, and it was too close to drive. She carried her purse with her and a copy of her application in a leather folio and nothing else. She wouldn't need her bag or anything from it. It would only be another weight on her shoulders.

She entered the building and walked up to the reception desk. This was going to be fine. It was an interview, not a trial. Nobody was there to play gotcha. She would answer their questions honestly. She would answer them thoroughly. She wouldn't obfuscate or lie. Then it would be out of her hands. They would recommend the best candidate that they had. Gwen hoped that it was her, but with the rumors going around, she could see why they would hesitate.

A quick conversation with a receptionist later, and Gwen stepped into an elevator that would take her to a level that consisted of conference rooms. When the elevator doors opened, she was faced with another receptionist. Another conversation and she was directed to a cluster of chairs where she could wait. She imagined her ten a.m. interview was the first of the day, but it was possible they had scheduled one before that. She would have to wait and see.

Gwen looked out the window to Atlanta sprawled beneath her, but she wasn't awed. It was nearly the same view she saw out of her own office window every day only at a slightly different angle.

She preferred the Atlanta she saw at night from the comfort of her condo's balcony.

At that moment, she knew that she was ready to move on from Dunleavy Byrd. If she didn't get the supreme court appointment, she didn't know what she'd do. Maybe she would start her own boutique appellate firm. It was too early to know right now. But she knew that it would be different from where she was right then.

"Ms. Strickland?" the receptionist said to get her attention. Gwen turned away from the window.

"Yes?" she asked politely. It never paid to be rude to the support staff.

"They're ready to see you. It's conference room C, just down that way." She motioned down the wide corridor. "I'll walk you back."

"Thank you." Gwen stood up and followed the receptionist back. The receptionist tapped on a closed door. They both heard a "Come in," and then she opened the door for Gwen.

"Good luck," the receptionist said, though Gwen knew it was probably pro forma. She would say the same thing to everyone who came by that day.

Gwen stepped into the conference room. There was a large, circular table studded with microphones and a video camera set up in the corner. Five people sat around the table. She already knew most of them, but they went through a round of introductions anyway. Then she was invited to take a seat. It was time for the interview to begin.

❖

Gwen surreptitiously glanced at her watch. They were coming up on the one-hour mark for the interview. So far, it had been incredibly thorough. They asked her about her current practice and her past practice. Someone had obviously done their research because they asked her about some of her earliest trials from before she had specialized in appellate law. They probed her reasoning on her writing sample, asking questions both about the substantive issues and why she had picked that sample in particular.

She did not tell them about Etta's involvement directly, but she did mention asking a colleague for her opinion.

They asked about statements that opposing counsel had submitted about her.

They asked about her son. They asked about her divorce.

After she answered all of those questions to the best of her ability, the interviewers shared a look, and the atmosphere in the room shifted.

"Ms. Strickland, we've heard some rumors about you in the legal community lately. Would you care to address them?" Judge Wilcox asked. It was a far more open-ended question than either she or Grey had anticipated, but she was still prepared.

She would tell the truth. She would say that the relationship should never have happened. She would say that it was a lapse in judgment, and it would never happen again. She would say Etta was a mistake, but that it wasn't indicative of her judgment. It had been one brief indiscretion and she had ended it.

She opened her mouth to start to do just that, but something stopped her. She closed her mouth.

She was supposed to be telling the truth, and none of that was true.

Oh, some of the details carried hints of the truth. She had ended the relationship, after all. But inside, in her conscience and in her heart, she knew that if she gave that answer, she would be lying.

The interviewers were looking at her intently. She knew she needed to say something even if she no longer knew what. She paused for another moment to gather herself before she started.

"I don't know exactly which rumors you've heard. I'm sure there are many variations going around, some of which are grounded in truth, and some of which aren't. Did I sleep with a subordinate? Yes, though she was never my direct report. I don't allow summer associates to work on my cases and I made no exceptions for her. Our relationship started before her employment at Dunleavy Byrd.

It ended temporarily when we first discovered we were working together, but we resumed it shortly thereafter." Gwen took a sip of the water that had been provided.

"I went over what I should say to this committee if the subject came up, and I was certain it would come up. I practiced my answer. I was going to tell you that I regretted the relationship, that it was a lapse in judgment." Gwen paused again. She steeled herself for what she was about to say next.

"I can't do that." She let the words sink in. The members of the committee shared another look. She ignored it.

"I can't tell you I regret something that I don't regret." She shook her head slightly. "You want me to say that it never should have started. I can't say that either.

"This interview rests on the assumption that I tell the truth, and to say those things would be to lie. I do not regret my relationship with Etta Monroe, and I will not tell you that I do, even if it costs me a supreme court seat. I only regret that it ended." Gwen folded her hands together on the table in front of her.

"I ended the relationship because I was more concerned about my career than what we had together. That was my mistake. That is what I need to apologize for. That was my lapse in judgment.

"I was going to say that I will not repeat my mistake and that I will not tarnish the reputation of this court. I can't say that either." She paused to gather her thoughts. "If I had the opportunity to resume that relationship, I would do so. Yes, she's a law student. Yes, she's sixteen years younger than me. I don't care.

"There is only one simple fact that matters: I love her."

Gwen took a deep, shuddering breath. "Do you need further clarification?"

Judge Wilcox looked like he didn't know what to say for a moment. The entire committee seemed taken aback. He quickly pulled himself together, though.

"No, I think you've covered the topic quite thoroughly." He coughed lightly, then he looked at the other committee members. "If no one has any further questions?"

The rest of the committee members indicated that they didn't want to ask her anything else. Judge Wilcox nodded and stood. Gwen took that as her cue to join him. Everyone else found their way to their feet, and she shook everyone's hand before Judge Wilcox escorted her out of the room.

"Thank you for coming by. Your interview was enlightening. You'll know our decision soon." Judge Wilcox offered her his hand again. They shook and after a few more pleasantries, Gwen headed to the elevator.

❖

"Well?" Grey stood up from the chair in the lobby where they were waiting. Gwen jumped.

"Christ, Grey. You'll kill me before they make a decision," Gwen said with a hand pressed to her chest. "What are you doing here?"

"You honestly expected me to wait for you to call me?" Grey looked at Gwen as if to say there was no way that was happening.

"I suppose not. Why don't you take me to lunch, and we can discuss everything there." Gwen gave Grey a pointed look. She was eating before she recounted the last hour of her life.

"Okay, I'll buy you lunch, but you'd better not skimp on the details." Grey took Gwen's arm and led her out of the building and down the street to the first lunch counter that they found. Then they dragged Gwen inside.

"Impatient much?" Gwen asked as she slid into a seat and Grey settled across from her.

"Incredibly." Grey tapped their fingers on the table. "Spill."

Gwen made Grey wait until after they ordered before she answered any of their questions. As soon as the server was gone, she slumped back in her seat. "I highly doubt I'll get the appointment." She waved a hand dismissively.

"What?" Grey furrowed their brow. "What do you mean? What went wrong?"

Gwen picked up her spoon, looked down at it, then deliberately placed it back on the table. "I couldn't do it."

"Couldn't do what?" Grey looked even more confused now than they had a second before.

"Everything we rehearsed about Etta. None of it was true. I couldn't say it." Gwen shrugged in resignation.

"Wait, what? We spent so long practicing those answers." Grey looked at Gwen like Gwen had lost her head.

"I don't..." Gwen tapped her fingers against the table. "I don't regret what happened with Etta, and I couldn't tell the interview committee that I did. It would have been a lie. I couldn't tell them I wouldn't do it again, because if I thought Etta would take me back, I would be all in. Telling them otherwise wouldn't have been right. I couldn't start my career as a supreme court justice by not telling the truth. I would rather not be appointed at all."

"That's..." Grey paused. "That's very noble of you. You've probably tanked your chances at a seat, but at least you did it for the right reasons."

"You're not disappointed?" Gwen asked cautiously.

Grey gave her a searching look. "Of course I'm not disappointed. I wanted it because you wanted it. I mean, it would have been cool to be friends with a supreme court justice, but as long as you're happy, I'm happy."

"I don't know that I would say happy, but I'm at peace with it," Gwen replied. "I miss her." She looked down at her hands, rubbing a thumb over the nail of the other thumb.

"I'm sorry." Grey reached out and took Gwen's hand. "I know that doesn't make you feel any better, but if I could fix it, I would."

"I know. I appreciate that," Gwen said. "I don't suppose you want to quit advocacy work and go back to being a real lawyer, do you?"

Grey looked at her suspiciously. "Not particularly, why?"

"After everything that happened at work, I don't know that I'm going to be there much longer."

"You're quitting? Or do you think they're going to fire you?" Grey's eyes narrowed.

"I don't see my future there anymore. I was thinking of starting my own appellate practice," Gwen said. "I haven't put much detailed thought into it yet, but I can't stay there."

"Gwen, I love you, but I am absolutely not quitting my job to come work for you. I love what I do too much," Grey replied.

Gwen laughed. "Fair enough. I didn't think that you'd say yes. And I suppose I can't really plan on anything until I find out if they're going to recommend me for the court and the governor makes a decision."

"So, what will you do in the meantime?" Grey tilted their head to the side in question.

"My contract says I have to give notice a month before I plan to leave. I'll do that today, I think. And if the appointment hasn't been made by the time the month is up, I might take some time off. Go on an adventure somewhere. Get out of Atlanta." Gwen didn't have any sort of definite plans yet. Everything hinged on the supreme court appointment.

"Well, I hope that either way, you can find a path that makes you happy. I still think it would be cool to know someone on the supreme court, though." Grey smiled.

"So, do I. I just wish Etta could be a part of it," Gwen said.

"You never know what might happen," Grey said as the server came back with their food.

Gwen tried not to let Grey's words get her hopes up, but life was strange. Maybe this wasn't the end after all.

Chapter Twenty-four

"Hey, Grey. What's up?" Etta answered her phone once she saw that Grey was the one calling her.

"Oh, just getting ready for the alliance's annual fundraising gala. I wanted to make sure you were planning on coming," Grey said.

"You know that I can't afford a ticket to the gala. And I'm sure I'll have to work that night," Etta objected. There were other reasons she wanted to avoid Atlanta and the gala too. The odds that Gwen would be there were high. She didn't want any sort of confrontation.

"You've put in more than enough sweat equity for me to comp you a ticket, and we both know you can take the night off if you want to," Grey replied. "I'm going to be incredibly upset if I don't see you there."

"And what are the odds Gwen will be there?" Etta asked. There was no sense in beating around the bush, not when they both knew why Etta was really avoiding the gala.

"Nearly one hundred percent. She provides fully a quarter of the alliance's annual budget. She would have to be in the hospital not to come," Grey said.

"Why isn't she on the board of directors?" Etta asked before she remembered she wasn't supposed to care.

"I tried, but she said the board had enough rich white people on it and it should represent the diversity of the communities we serve. So she told me to put someone from an underrepresented group on the board instead. When someone funnels as much money into a group as she does, you do what she wants," Grey replied.

"That's…" Etta said.

"Idealistic," Grey supplied. "She likes to lean into the rich bitch thing, but she certainly has her beliefs, and she sticks by them. Sometimes at great personal sacrifice."

"You make her sound very noble," Etta said. "I wish that had been my experience."

"You should talk to her. You should ask her about her supreme court interview," Grey said.

"Why would I do that?" Etta asked. "I'm sure she did a great job, but I don't see what that has to do with anything."

"I know you're skeptical, and I can't tell you why you should talk to her. That's up to you and Gwen, but you should give her the chance to talk to you about it. Anyway, you should also come to the gala. I didn't get to see you as much this summer as I would have liked," Grey prodded. "Plus, I want to show you off to the other donors. You're probably our most involved volunteer, and people should know that. I'm sending you a ticket and putting you on the guest list. All you have to do is show up."

"I'll think about it," Etta replied. Grey certainly hadn't made the decision to attend an easy one. It would be much easier to avoid Gwen if she didn't go, but after what Grey had hinted at, did she want to avoid Gwen? She wasn't sure.

"That's all I can ask for. Now, enjoy the beginning of your last year in law school. You only get to do it once."

Etta laughed. "I'll try. Have a good night."

"You too."

Etta hung up the phone and then pinched the bridge of her nose. She would need to decide soon to make sure she'd have something to wear. She wasn't the sort of person who had gala-ready attire in her closet. She would have to go shopping. When had her life gotten so complicated?

❖

Gwen slipped the dark purple silk down her body, then grabbed the zipper on the side of the dress before slowly zipping it up her side. She turned toward the mirror and smoothed the front of the dress down.

"You're taking forever," came Grey's voice from the other side of the dressing room door.

Gwen laughed. She gave the dress another look before she opened the door and presented herself to Grey and to the attendant helping them.

"Just because you were happy with the first thing you tried on doesn't mean we're all going to be that lucky," Gwen said, as she stepped out of the room and toward the three-way mirror.

"What can I say, some of us aren't overly picky." Grey had their hands in their pockets as they leaned against the outside wall of the dressing room. "You look spectacular."

"Thank you." Gwen stood between the mirrors and gave herself a critical look. The dress flattered her figure and hugged her curves. The color was perfect. She was incredibly pleased.

"You know, Etta's probably going to be at the gala."

Gwen furrowed her eyebrows. "She is?" Galas of any sort didn't seem to be Etta's scene, but then, maybe they were. Maybe Gwen was underestimating her.

"She's our best, most involved law student volunteer. I gave her a ticket," Grey said.

Gwen narrowed her eyes. "Really? So, there was no ulterior motive on your part?"

"Of course there was an ulterior motive. I think it would be good for the two of you to talk again." Grey looked at Gwen pointedly.

"Since when are you in favor of this relationship? You're the one who told me I should never see her again."

"That was before you told me you loved her. You know I'm a romantic at heart," Grey said.

"You're a lothario at heart!" Having seen enough of the dress, she walked back into the dressing room to start taking it off.

"That's only when it comes to my life. But deep down, you

want to be happily monogamous with your scandalously young lover, and I support that," Grey said over the dressing room wall.

"There's a difference between supporting and interfering," Gwen replied.

"I don't know what you're talking about." Grey tapped a nail against the door impatiently.

"Yes, you do. Promise me you're not going to lock us together in a coat closet. In fact, promise me that you're not going to lock us together anywhere." Gwen unzipped the dress and slid it off.

"I promise, no coat closets. No locks." Gwen listened as Grey paced a few steps away from the dressing room.

"Thank you." She hung the dress back up on its hanger and started to put her own clothing back on.

"But I still think you should find some time to talk to her," Grey said.

"We'll see," Gwen replied, though she knew she would probably spend all night avoiding Etta instead. She had treated Etta so badly. Surely, Etta had no desire to talk to her. Still, apologizing didn't sound like the worst idea in the world. If Etta would allow her to. It was something to think about.

Gwen pushed open the dressing room door. "I'm taking the purple one," she said to the attendant, then she turned to Grey. "All right. I'm ready to go when you are."

"Finally," Grey said and exhaled. "I need you to buy me coffee before you start talking about shoes, though."

"All right, I'll buy you some coffee." Gwen looked at Grey indulgently and looped her arm through theirs. "Lead the way."

Chapter Twenty-five

Etta handed her car over to the valet outside the old theater and tried not to feel self-conscious. There was no way her little Hyundai fit in with all of the other cars the valet had probably seen that night. He grinned at her anyway when he took her car, so she thought maybe he understood her plight.

Her sparkly red dress felt foreign against her skin. It was heavier than she anticipated when she tried it on, the sequins giving it a weight she hadn't thought about when she had looked at fancy dresses on the red carpet on TV. It did make the dress drape nicely, though.

She stepped inside the theater and was immediately presented with a sign welcoming the guests. She was probably too early, but it was hard to time the drive from Cartersville. She saw a table set up to the side with a person manning it, so she headed in that direction. As she got close, she took her phone out of her clutch and pulled up her ticket.

"Hi," she said to the person at the table, her stomach swooping with nerves. She got a quiet greeting in return. She held her phone out and he scanned the ticket, then he checked her name against the guest list.

"You're all set. Enjoy your night." He waved her through the entryway.

Etta said, "Thank you," before she stepped under an archway made of rainbow balloons. She would have been more comfortable at the table taking tickets, but Grey hadn't given her that option.

She stepped into the still sparsely populated theater and looked around. A dance floor. A silent auction. High-top tables around the perimeter. Several spread-out tables of hors d'oeuvres. An art deco–styled bar with numerous bartenders at the back of the room. It all looked very elegant, with more colorful balloons everywhere, and streamers. The tables had floral centerpieces. It all went together nicely, but it was all pretty standard, as these things went. She had never been to something with a live jazz band before. They weren't playing yet, but she assumed they would start once the night picked up steam.

She didn't know what to do with herself. None of the people floating around looked familiar to her, and Grey was nowhere to be seen. She headed toward the bar. That seemed like a safe enough bet, and she was sure it would be incredibly busy later.

As she reached the bar, Grey seemingly appeared out of nowhere. "You're here!" they exclaimed. Grey leaned in and pulled Etta into a hug. It was somewhat out of character. Grey had never particularly given off the vibe that they were a hugger, but they didn't seem drunk, just buzzed on too much caffeine. Etta returned the hug.

"You know, I could have taken tickets tonight, or worked the bar, or done something to help," Etta said to the jittery-looking Grey.

"Don't be ridiculous. This is supposed to be a reward for all of the hard work you do. You can't relax if I make you do more work. Besides, the ticket taker works for the theater, and the bartenders are employed by the caterer. I've got someone manning the silent auction already. Your services aren't needed." Grey flagged down a bartender. When the bartender arrived, Grey told him, "She's going to have a glass of prosecco on me," before motioning to Etta.

"Coming right up." He spun around and grabbed one of the many bottles of prosecco from a bucket of ice on top of the back bar, quickly disposing of the foil around the neck, and popping it open with no problems. A few seconds later, he was placing the drink on the bar in front of Etta. "Cheers."

Etta picked the flute up and took a sip, letting the cool, sparkly wine linger in her mouth for a second. She relaxed slightly.

"I need to go see to a few more details, but you should mingle. Go meet some people. If you feel like it, talk about all of the work you do for the alliance. That can be your contribution for the night." Grey smiled a winning smile, and Etta understood how they managed to charm donations out of people.

"I'll do that. Thank you for the drink." Etta couldn't help but smile back. Maybe this wouldn't be such a bad experience after all. If she could avoid Gwen, then maybe she could enjoy herself. She was curious about what Grey had meant when they had told her to ask Gwen about her interview, but not curious enough to seek her out. She had tried that already. Gwen had kicked her out. She wasn't going to risk another confrontation, particularly not in public.

Etta turned back to the theater's open space and decided that talking to strangers wouldn't hurt her. She talked to strangers at the bar all the time. She could always check out the silent auction even if she couldn't afford to bid on anything.

❖

Gwen finally managed to extract herself from the conversation with a state representative that she hadn't wanted to have in the first place. He was fishing for donations, and she wasn't interested in providing one. Yes, he voted in favor of gay rights when the issue came up, but she wasn't even in his district. She wasn't going to give money to every Democratic elected official in the state. His reelection was almost assured. There were better places for her to funnel her money.

She looked around to locate the people she most wanted to avoid, so she could go in the other direction. The side area where they were conducting the silent auction seemed to be safe. She headed toward it.

The tables were set up with gift baskets and displays with bidding sheets in front of each one. She didn't expect to find anything that she was particularly interested in. Gift cards to boutiques she didn't shop at. Plastic surgery deals that she avoided entirely. She paused briefly at a package of Braves tickets. Christian liked baseball. She wrote down a bid, but not one designed to categorically prevent other people from bidding. If she won, she'd happily pay the price, but she wasn't going to obsess over it.

She kept going down the line. More things she wasn't interested in.

When she got to the last table, she stopped. It was a trip for two to Sint Maarten. It wasn't quite Antigua, but it was the same idea. She hadn't taken a vacation in years. She might not have anyone to go with, but she was sure she could drag Grey along. Her last month at Dunleavy Byrd would be over soon enough, then she would have plenty of free time while she decided what she wanted to do next. She could think about that from a Caribbean beach just as well as she could from Atlanta. She wrote down a number that far exceeded the value of the package. Not the best strategy from a financial point of view, but hopefully it meant that no one else would bid on it. She could feel the sea air already.

She stepped away from the table and straight into Etta.

❖

Etta pulled up short when Gwen suddenly appeared in front of her. Her mind went blank. The only thing she could think to say was, "Gwen."

"Etta." Gwen stood up a little straighter. "I…"

Etta waited for Gwen to say something, but it seemed like nothing was going to be forthcoming.

"I was just"—Etta weakly pointed past Gwen—"heading to the bar."

Gwen looked over her shoulder as if she had forgotten where the bar was. "Of course." She stepped aside so Etta could resume her mission.

As Etta stepped past Gwen, her stomach churned.

She was half a step away when she heard Gwen say her name one more time. She turned around and waited for Gwen to say something.

"I'm sorry." It looked like the words had escaped from Gwen's mouth more than that she had intended to say them.

"That's…" Etta didn't know what to say. She stood there looking at Gwen for a long moment. She eventually came up with, "Thank you." It was good to hear Gwen apologize—to acknowledge that she had done something wrong. Etta hadn't thought she'd get that if they spoke to each other again.

"Gwen, there you are," a voice said from behind Etta. "I'm sorry to interrupt, but I've been trying to get you alone all night and I'm about to leave."

Etta watched as the woman walked past her and up to Gwen. It took Etta a minute to realize that the woman was the governor. She thought that she should probably walk away, but she was too curious to hear what the governor was going to say to leave.

"What can I do for you, Governor?" Gwen took the hand that was extended in her direction. She looked confused, and Etta wondered why.

"I wanted to let you know that I watched your interview, and I was very impressed with your commitment to the truth," the governor said. "It seems I've got a job opening to fill. I can't say anything directly, but you should know that your application is being considered very seriously."

If anything, Gwen looked even more confused. "Thank you, ma'am. That's good to know." She blinked a little too rapidly, as if she was trying to figure something out.

If Gwen was confused, Etta was bewildered. Before she could come to any sort of conclusion, the governor turned to her.

"I wish I had someone as devoted to me as she is to you. I hope you know how lucky you are." The governor put a hand on Etta's forearm and squeezed it before she stepped away from the pair of them.

Etta looked at Gwen in bafflement. Gwen's cheeks had a pink tinge to them, and she looked uncomfortable. Before Etta could ask any of the myriad questions she had, Gwen shook herself out of her stupor and said, "I need to go."

She turned on her heel and walked in the opposite direction even though she had just come from that way.

Between what Grey had said, and what the governor had just revealed, Etta needed to know what Gwen had said in her interview. The committee members were sworn to keep the interview confidential. There was only one person who could answer her questions. Gwen.

And Gwen was walking away.

Chapter Twenty-six

"Have you seen Gwen?" Etta asked when she ran into Grey by the bar. She wanted answers, but she couldn't find Gwen anywhere.

Grey looked around as if to make sure Etta hadn't simply overlooked her. "Not recently. I can call her for you."

"No. That's okay. I'll keep looking." Etta pursed her lips in annoyance. It figured that Gwen would disappear as soon as Etta wanted to have a conversation. She looked around the room once again. Maybe Gwen was in the bathroom.

❖

Gwen stepped out onto the terrace. It wasn't easily seen from inside, but she had been to the venue before and knew it was there. After the governor's pronouncement, she needed some time to get her thoughts straight. If her location made it harder for Etta to find her and demand answers, so much the better.

Seeing Etta again had brought a rush of feeling to her chest. One brief interaction was enough for Gwen to want to do more than simply apologize. She wanted to ask Etta to take her back. That wouldn't be fair to Etta, though.

Gwen knew her actions had been wrong. She never should have made Etta leave, but she had done it. It was in the past now. There was no sense in dragging it all back up only for Etta tell her that she never wanted to see her again.

And Etta didn't deserve to have Gwen drag up the past just to make herself feel better. She had apologized already. It was better to let the past remain in the past.

❖

Etta stepped out of the theater and looked for the valet. He wasn't there, but that wasn't surprising. Other people were leaving as well, and he was probably getting someone else's car. After standing almost all night, she was happy to sink down onto a bench. She stretched her legs out in front of her and took a deep breath as she arched her back. She wasn't looking forward to driving back to Cartersville so late at night. She'd stayed later than she had intended, looking for Gwen to have a conversation with her, but it was like Gwen had completely vanished. Maybe she had simply left the fundraiser altogether.

Etta groaned when her phone rang. There weren't that many people who would call her at close to midnight. That list was either Jorge asking her to drive him home after having too much to drink, or her mom. Jorge was back in Cartersville and knew she wasn't in town, so it had to be her mom. She thought about not answering it at all, but that would be more grief in the end than it was worth to temporarily avoid a conversation.

She pulled her phone out of her clutch. It was Grey. She swiped her phone to answer it, wondering what Grey could possibly want with her. Maybe they needed someone to help break things down. Etta lifted the phone to her ear.

"Hello?"

"Hey, have you left yet? Like, are you on the road?" Grey asked with urgency in their voice.

"No. I'm sitting outside waiting on the valet. Why?" It had already been a confusing night for Etta and Grey was only making it more so.

"I've got a donor I want you to talk to. I think I might be able to squeeze a bigger donation from her if she talks to someone who's been out there doing the work. Can you meet us at the Painted Fish Diner? It's a five-minute drive away," Grey said.

"Uh, sure," Etta replied. If it was a big enough deal for Grey to call her when she might be halfway back to Cartersville, then Etta would do it.

"Just grab a table. We should be there in twenty minutes, tops. I've got to wrap up a few things here before I can get over there." Grey certainly made it sound important.

"Okay. I'll see you there." Etta rubbed the back of her neck. Hopefully this conversation wouldn't take too long. She did still have to drive back to Cartersville, and she didn't want to be doing it at four a.m.

"Awesome. Thanks." Grey hung up before Etta could respond. The valet arrived with someone's car, and after returning it to them, he took Etta's ticket to get hers.

❖

"To a successful night." Gwen raised her glass of prosecco in Grey's direction. Grey looked exhausted but pleased.

"Very successful." Grey clinked their glass against Gwen's. "I'm going to sleep for a week, but first I need pancakes."

"I will never understand your need to eat breakfast after these things." Gwen smiled at Grey's predictability.

"You don't have to understand it. You just have to support it. You're coming, right?" Grey asked. They pinned Gwen with a look that said there was only one right answer.

"Of course I'm coming. I'm not going to send you off alone to some random diner at midnight. You might not make it home." Gwen returned Grey's look.

"I'm not going to get attacked between here and the diner," Grey said wryly.

"I didn't say you would. But it would be just like you to run into someone attractive at said diner, and then you wouldn't sleep for days," Gwen teased.

"Fine. You're right." Grey threw up the hand that wasn't holding their prosecco. "Let's grab our stuff and get out of here."

❖

Etta blew on her cup of coffee before taking a sip. She checked the time on her phone. Grey had said twenty minutes. It had been fifteen. Still, Etta was getting antsy. The coffee would help her stay awake for the drive, but it was still getting late.

Etta looked up as the bell over the door rang. She sighed in relief when she saw Grey. Then she looked to see who the donor might be.

Gwen.

It was Gwen standing with Grey at the door. Gwen couldn't possibly be the donor Grey had told her about. That didn't make sense.

Gwen made eye contact with her, then said something to Grey. Etta wasn't proficient in lip reading, so she didn't know what it was or what Grey said in return. Whatever it was, it got Gwen moving in her direction. Grey walked behind her.

They stopped when they got to Etta's table.

"Grey, what's going on?" Etta asked as she looked between the two of them. Had Gwen asked Grey to lure her to the diner?

"The two of you need to talk." Grey motioned between the two of them. "You"—they pointed at Etta—"were trying to find Gwen for half of the night. And you"—they turned to Gwen—"have been moping for weeks. Now I've provided the venue. Get everything out of your systems." Grey looked between them significantly. "While you do that, I am going to be by the door eating some of the best pancakes in Atlanta." Grey stepped away from the table and shooed Gwen toward it.

Gwen huffed at Grey's antics and watched them as they retreated to the front of the diner, then she turned back to Etta. She closed her eyes briefly, and Etta wondered what she was thinking about. When she opened them, she looked at Etta directly. "May I sit down?"

Etta looked back at her, trying to gauge what she might have to say. The problem was, she had no idea. The only way she could find out would be to let Gwen join her. She could get her questions answered, though. And she really wanted answers.

"Yeah, sure." Etta nodded toward the other side of the booth. Gwen slid into it.

Chapter Twenty-seven

I should apologize again," Gwen said after a minute of silence. Etta had been waiting for her to go first. She wanted to see what Gwen had to say for herself.

"Yeah." Etta swallowed. "You should." She wouldn't let Gwen off the hook just because she had some questions.

"I'm sorry. I put keeping my job ahead of our relationship, and I should have realized that we were more important than a job. I know I hurt you, and I regret that. If I could do it differently, I would." Gwen clasped her hands together and rubbed her thumb over the nail of her other thumb.

"How would you do it differently?" Etta needed to know before she could move past the hurt Gwen had put her through.

"I wouldn't have treated you like a liability. I wouldn't have pushed you away. If it had come down to it, I would have walked away from the job in order to keep you." Gwen looked at Etta intently, as if trying to predict how Etta would react.

"I appreciate you telling me that." Etta wrapped her hands around her coffee mug. She looked down into it as if the liquid could give her some insight into what was going on. She knew she wouldn't get anything from the coffee, though. She looked back up again. "What did the governor mean when she said I should know how lucky I am? How did she know who I am to you?" Etta couldn't hold back her curiosity anymore.

Etta never thought she would see Gwen squirm, but Gwen

certainly looked uncomfortable now. "It's not important," she tried to deflect.

"Clearly, it is." Etta looked at Gwen pointedly. "Tell me what she meant. What happened in your interview? Grey told me to ask you, and after the governor's comment—" Etta shrugged helplessly. "I need you to tell me what happened."

Gwen rubbed her forehead then met Etta's eyes. "I told the committee that I loved you."

"I'm sorry, what?" Gwen couldn't have said what Etta thought she said. "Why…" She paused to pull her thoughts together. "Why would you do that? How was that even relevant?"

"At the end of the interview, they asked me about our relationship. I assume they expected that I would disavow it. That I would say that it was a mistake and that I regretted it." Gwen shifted her shoulders. "I couldn't do that." She looked away for a few seconds then looked back at Etta. "I couldn't do that and tell the truth. And I wasn't prepared to accept a seat on the supreme court if it was contingent on telling a lie. I couldn't lie about you. I felt…I *feel*…I couldn't deny that. I couldn't deny what we had, what you meant to me. So I told them the truth. They recorded the interview. I assume the governor watched the tape." Gwen looked down at her hands where they rested on the table top.

"You told them—" Etta put her fingers over her eyes, rubbed them, then opened them again. Gwen had given up a supreme court seat for her. It was inconceivable. No one did that. Yet Gwen had done it. For her. Because she loved her.

"That's why I didn't want to tell you what happened. It isn't fair of me to tell you that I love you now. Not after everything I did to you." Gwen curled her fingers in on each other.

"Christ, you're an idiot," Etta muttered. "You should not have done that. You should not have given up a supreme court seat for me. You could have found something else to say. I'm not—Christ. We're leaving now." Etta started to slide to the edge of the bench.

"We are?" Gwen looked at Etta as if Etta had suddenly gone crazy.

"Yes, we are. We're going back to your condo. I need someplace private to yell at you for doing something so boneheadedly stupid, and then I'm going to kiss you senseless. This diner isn't an appropriate place to do either of those things, so, yes, we're leaving." Standing now, Etta held a hand out for Gwen to take.

Gwen looked up at Etta in awe for a split second before she reached out and put her hand in Etta's. With a tug, Etta pulled Gwen to her feet and then toward the front of the diner. As they approached Grey's table, Gwen pulled Etta to a stop. Etta looked back at her curiously.

"Your pancakes are on me," Gwen said as she pulled some cash out of her clutch and dropped it on Grey's table.

Grey laughed uproariously as Etta grabbed Gwen's hand again and pulled her from the diner.

They got as far as Etta's car before Etta pressed Gwen against the side of it. Once she had Gwen where she wanted her, she leaned in and kissed her. The kiss was hard and long, and Etta felt the moment Gwen melted into it. After a minute, Etta pulled away. "Just to be clear, I love you too, though I'm going to need you to tell *me* that you love me, and not a committee full of strangers."

Gwen brought her hands up to cup Etta's face. "I love you." She leaned in to kiss her again. This kiss was softer, but it lingered. Eventually, Gwen ended it. "I thought we were waiting until we got back to my place before we did that."

"Oh, I still intend to yell at you once we get there. This is just a preview of what's going to come afterward." Etta laughed. She placed another fleeting kiss on Gwen's lips. "Now, get in the car."

EPILOGUE

G wen beamed at Christian as the two of them walked to the lectern in the well of the Georgia House Chambers. The governor awaited them. She also had a smile on her face, and she shook Gwen's hand once Gwen got close enough.

Christian held the Bible between the two of them, and Gwen paused for a moment before she placed her hand on it. Was she ready to do this? It only took a second for her to find the answer. Yes. She was ready. She raised her right hand and looked at the governor.

"I, Gwendolyn Abigail Strickland, do solemnly swear—" Gwen tried not to rush through the oath, but it was over before she realized it.

"Congratulations, Justice," the governor said as she shook Gwen's hand again. As soon as the handshake was over, Gwen turned to Christian and hugged him, leaving a kiss on his cheek. After that, she found Etta sitting in one of the closer seats to the center of the chambers. They made eye contact before Gwen forced herself to look away. She had a speech to give, after all.

❖

"Thank you." Gwen ended her speech at the lectern and closed her leather folio. Everyone in the chambers stood and applauded. Etta had never expected to experience anything like it. In no world was she supposed to be at the swearing in of a Georgia Supreme Court Justice. Or at least she was supposed to be long out of law school before it happened. But here she was, clapping, as the love of her life ascended to the bench of the highest court in the state of Georgia. She wondered if she could get Gwen to swear her into the bar after she passed the bar exam. Would that be a conflict of interest? She would have to ask.

❖

Gwen stretched out in her beach chair. She reached her arm out and brushed her fingers against Etta's arm to get her attention. Etta turned her face in Gwen's direction.

"Hmm?" Etta looked at Gwen through her sunglasses. From what Gwen could tell, she was perfectly relaxed.

"Are you having a good vacation?" Gwen asked.

"Is this where you say I told you so? Because I'm not interested in hearing it." Etta lazily turned her head back toward the water.

"You have to admit that Sint Maarten is gorgeous," Gwen prodded.

"I'm sure there would have been gorgeous places in the United States too. I'm clearly here under extreme protest." Etta could barely keep the smile from her face.

The supreme court oral argument calendar had paused for the winter holidays, and Gwen couldn't think of anywhere else she wanted to be. Really, she would have been content to stay in Georgia if Etta had wanted to, but once she had told Etta that she had already paid for the vacation, Etta's complaints had disappeared.

"I can send you back to the US, you know," Gwen said.

"You won't," Etta replied. "You like the sight of me in a bikini too much."

At that, Gwen let her eyes travel down Etta's body, then back to her face. "You're right. I do like that. I suppose you can stay."

Gwen knew Etta had to be rolling her eyes even if she couldn't see it.

"If it pleases the court," Etta said with heavy sarcasm as she stood up. "I'm going to go get in the shower. It's almost time for dinner. You should come with me." Etta held a hand out to Gwen.

"If I do that, we'll never get to dinner," she replied, but she took Etta's hand anyway. Once they were both standing, she leaned in for a kiss. Etta gave her one without further protest.

"I'm willing to risk that. Come inside. We'll get around to dinner eventually." Etta tugged Gwen after her. Gwen happily followed Etta back to their room. She would follow Etta anywhere.

About the Author

Ashley Moore lives in Charleston, South Carolina, with her dog, Tallulah. She went to college in Georgia and law school in Virginia, and has lived in seven states in the last fifteen years. Her interests include craft cocktails and woodworking. She is a finalist for several Golden Crown Literary Society awards including Best New Author. She can be found on Instagram at leaping_waters and emailed at Ashley@AshleyMooreWrites.com.

Books Available From Bold Strokes Books

A Case for Discretion by Ashley Moore. Will Gwen, a prominent Atlanta attorney, choose Etta, the law student she's clandestinely dating, or is her political future too important to sacrifice? (978-1-63679-617-8)

Aubrey McFadden Is Never Getting Married by Georgia Beers. Aubrey McFadden is never getting married, but she does have five weddings to attend, and she'll be avoiding Monica Wallace, the woman who ruined her happily ever after, at every single one. (978-1-63679-613-0)

The Broken Lines of Us by Shia Woods. Charlie Dawson returns to the city she left behind and meets an unexpected stranger on her first night back, discovering that coming home might not be as hard as she thought. (978-1-63679-585-0)

Flowers for Dead Girls by Abigail Collins. Isla might be just the right kind of girl to bring Astra out of her shell—and maybe more. The only problem? She's dead. (978-1-63679-584-3)

Good Bones by Aurora Rey. Designer and contractor Logan Barrow can give Kathleen Kenney the house of her dreams, but can she convince the cynical romance writer to take a chance on love? (978-1-63679-589-8)

Leather, Lace, and Locs by Anne Shade. Three friends, each on their own path in life, with one obstacle…finding room in their busy lives for a love that will give them their happily ever afters. (978-1-63679-529-4)

Rainbow Overalls by Maggie Fortuna. Arriving in Vermont for her first year of college, an introverted bookworm forms a friendship with an outgoing artist and finds what comes after the classic coming out story: a being out story. (978-1-63679-606-2)

Revisiting Summer Nights by Ashley Bartlett. PJ Addison and Wylie Parsons have been called back to film the most recent *Dangerous Summer Nights* installment. Only this time they're not in love, and it's going to stay that way. (978-1-63679-551-5)

All This Time by Sage Donnell. Erin and Jodi share a complicated past, but a very different present. Will they ever be able to make a future together work? (978-1-63679-622-2)

Crossing Bridges by Chelsey Lynford. When a one-night stand between a snowboard instructor and a business executive becomes more, one has to overcome her past, while the other must let go of her planned future. (978-1-63679-646-8)

Dancing Toward Stardust by Julia Underwood. Age has nothing to do with becoming the person you were meant to be, taking a chance, and finding love. (978-1-63679-588-1)

Evacuation to Love by CA Popovich. As a hurricane rips through Florida, so too are Joanne and Shanna's lives upended. It'll take a force of nature to show them the love it takes to rebuild. (978-1-63679-493-8)

Lean in to Love by Catherine Lane. Will badly behaving celebrities, erotic sex tapes, and steamy scandals prevent Rory and Ellis from leaning in to love? (978-1-63679-582-9)

The Romance Lovers Book Club by MA Binfield and Toni Logan. After their book club reads a romance about an American tourist falling in love with an English princess, Harper and her best friend, Alice, book an impulsive trip to London hoping they'll both fall for the women of their dreams. (978-1-63679-501-0)

Searching for Someday by Renee Roman. For loner Rayne Thomas, her only goal for working out is to build her confidence, but Maggie Flanders has another idea, and neither is prepared for the outcome. (978-1-63679-568-3)

Truly Home by J.J. Hale. Ruth and Olivia discover home is more than a four-letter word. (978-1-63679-579-9)

View from the Top by Morgan Adams. When it comes to love, some-times the higher you climb, the harder you fall. (978-1-63679-604-8)

Blood Rage by Illeandra Young. A stolen artifact, a family in the dark, an entire city on edge. Can SPEAR agent Danika Karson juggle all three over a weekend with the "in-laws" while an unknown, malevolent entity lies in wait upon her very skin? (978-1-63679-539-3)

Ghost Town by R.E. Ward. Blair Wyndon and Leif Henderson are set to prove ghosts exist when the mystery suddenly turns deadly. Someone or something else is in Masonville, and if they don't find a way to escape, they might never leave. (978-1-63679-523-2)

Good Christian Girls by Elizabeth Bradshaw. In this heartfelt coming of age lesbian romance, Lacey and Jo help each other untangle who they are from who everyone says they're supposed to be. (978-1-63679-555-3)

Guide Us Home by CF Frizzell and Jesse J. Thoma. When acquisition of an abandoned lighthouse pits ambitious competitors Nancy and Sam against each other, it takes a WWII tale of two brave women to make them see the light. (978-1-63679-533-1)

Lost Harbor by Kimberly Cooper Griffin. For Alice and Bridget's love to survive, they must find a way to reconcile the most important passions in their lives—devotion to the church and each other. (978-1-63679-463-1)

Never a Bridesmaid by Spencer Greene. As her sister's wedding gets closer, Jessica finds that her hatred for the maid of honor is a bit more complicated than she thought. Could it be something more than hatred? (978-1-63679-559-1)

The Rewind by Nicole Stiling. For police detective Cami Lyons and crime reporter Alicia Flynn, some choices break hearts. Others leave a body count. (978-1-63679-572-0)

Turning Point by Cathy Dunnell. When Asha and her former high school bully Jody struggle to deny their growing attraction, can they move forward without going back? (978-1-63679-549-2)

When Tomorrow Comes by D. Jackson Leigh. Teague Maxwell, convinced she will die before she turns 41, hires animal rescue owner Baye Cobb to rehome her extensive menagerie. (978-1-63679-557-7)

You Had Me at Merlot by Melissa Brayden. Leighton and Jamie have all the ingredients to turn their attraction into love, but it's a recipe for disaster.(978-1-63679-543-0)